WITCH OF WINTER

WITCH OF WINTER

by
Robert F. Bollendorf, Ed.D., CADC
and
Donna J. Gluck, MS, LCPC

College of DuPage Press
First Edition

WITCH OF WINTER
By Robert F. Bollendorf, Ed.D., CADC & Donna J. Gluck, MS, LCPC

Edited by Eleanor Donlon & William Makely
Front cover design by Jennifer Holman
Book typography and back cover design by Janice Walker

College of DuPage Press
425 Fawell Boulevard
Glen Ellyn, IL 60137
800-290-4474
www.dupagepress.com

ISBN 978-1-932514-22-3

Dedicated to my boys: Jason, Erick, Jalen, and Jeffery
For keeping me young at heart and in spirit.
With love,
Nana Donna

acknowledgments

ONCE AGAIN, WE WOULD like to thank the Menominee people, especially the historical society, members of the tribal police department, and the staff of Maehnowesekiyah. Maehnowesekiyah is a real treatment center and we visited it to get information about treatment. It would be impossible in our brief visit to learn all the aspects of treatment; therefore we do not even pretend that what is described in this book is what actually transpires there. Plus, it should be noted that most treatment centers have moved away from the cookie-cutter approach of the early days of treatment. Today, patients each receive an individual treatment plan.

Many of the same people involved in this book have helped us with each of the previous books. Thank you all for your continued help and support. We would especially like to thank Tom Richardson for his input on cross-country skiing and winter camping. Tom and Rob have been friends for many years and have had a number of wilderness adventures together, so his counsel and advice in those areas have spanned a number of decades.

Our special thanks also go to April Hanstad, who has worked tirelessly on improving the quality of these books. There are hundreds of details that would have been missed if not for her. Thanks too to Joe Barillari for his efforts to make this a quality product, and also for his faith in us as writers and willingness to take a risk on our behalf. Thanks to readers and editors, especially Dave Luce, William Makely, Eleanor Donlon, and Sharon Andersohn.

Heartfelt thanks to Nick and Charlotte Hockings and their three beautiful grandchildren. We have been lovingly welcomed into their home, hearts, and traditional teachings. They have not only supported our work; much was inspired by them all.

Donna would also like to thank her husband, Jeff, for his encouragement and understanding as writing took time away from "family." Lastly, a loving thank you to her parents, Betty and Harry, who taught her a love and respect for nature along with inspiring her to try and try again!

LUCY TELLER WONDERED at first if she were dreaming when she saw the girl kneeling by a tree in a foot of new snow.

It was the middle of a brutally cold February. Lucy had been lost in thought as her squad car drove itself along Highway 55. She should have been paying more attention; there had been a major snowstorm the night before, and the roads were still white with snow. It was one of those surprising snowfalls that started gently and turned into a major snow event—the kind Lucy liked to walk through after dark. The temperature was in the mid-twenties, and there was no wind. She expected, when it started, that it would snow an inch or two, but she was too optimistic. Now it was beginning to taper off, but not before it had dropped nearly a foot on top of the several inches already on the ground.

Lucy, still the new kid in the department, was working the day shift on a Sunday for the Menominee Tribal Police. It was early morning just past dawn, and with the snow that meant that the headlights didn't work quite as well. She had just driven past Spirit Rock, sitting back in the woods and covered by a blanket of fresh snow.

Lucy began daydreaming about the legend of the rock. It was said that a group of hunters approached the god, Nanabush, to ask for improved hunting skills. Nanabush was impressed with their courage in approaching him, especially since he wasn't known for his kindness toward humans, and granted them their wish. Then one of the group members pressed his luck even further and had the audacity to ask for eternal life. This angered Nanabush. He pushed the man to the ground and turned him into a rock saying, "Now you have eternal life." It was believed among the Menominees that if the rock ever crumbled, the tribe would cease to exist.

Lucy wondered if the rock still had the spirit and feeling of a man and, if so, whether he liked the new snow covering him and appreciated the extra protection from the sub-zero temperatures that always followed a heavy snow in northern Wisconsin. She was glad, too, that the legend wasn't that the burying of the rock signaled the demise of the tribe since the rock had been buried every winter for as long as she could remember.

Winter was certainly a good description of the current state of the tribe: it was covered and surrounded by white. It was estimated that the Menominee tribe had been in existence for ten thousand years, and they once owned nearly ten million acres of land. Since 1634, when the Menominee met Jean Nicolet, the "first" white man, their land had shrunk to about two hundred thirty thousand acres. If it weren't for Chief Oshkosh's refusal to move, they would be in Minnesota somewhere, blended with other tribes.

As it was, they had lost much of their history. Children attended mission schools and the elders were discouraged from passing on tribal history and tradition to their young. Still, the Menominee preserved the land in their charge. Ninety-five percent still produced hardwood, pine, and hemlock trees. Lucy was lost in wonder as she drove, admiring all of the large trees in their winter slumber and covered with a fresh coat of white. She was traveling next to the twenty-four miles of Wolf River that still ran through Menominee land. Lucy thought of the dams that had been built upstream. Because of them, the Menominee's brother, the sturgeon, was no longer able to visit Keshena Falls in the spring to spawn.

Still, it was impossible for Lucy to think what her life might be like had none of that taken place. Change had come, and the Menominee had to adjust, hopefully keeping their culture alive as well.

She was passing near the tree where Scott Brandt had been killed. It was only a few weeks after the resolution of the case. His two murderers were now in jail and hopefully would stay there a long time. The Brandt case had captured Lucy's imagination even before it was acknowledged as a case by the rest of her department. To most people, Scott was just a drug addict and crash victim. To her, the mystery of his death and of his life had been something more. Lucy wondered once again why she had gotten so caught up in helping a white man she had thought she had only met in the dark of a sweat lodge.

That's when she saw the tiny figure kneeling by the tree— Scott's tree. Because of the deep snow, she couldn't pull her squad car completely off the road. She wasn't sure at first if it was a girl or just a trick played on her eyes by the falling snow. She slowed and peered more closely. There *was* a girl.

With a strange feeling of déjà vu, Lucy stopped the car. The girl didn't hear her approach. Lucy was concerned about startling her, but she had to turn on her dome lights. The girl turned immediately, looked at the car, and began to run into the woods.

Lucy got out hurriedly from her squad car. She looked again, carefully and keenly, and, with a start, recognized the girl. Then she understood the feeling of déjà vu. She had seen the girl there once before.

"Lisa," she called. "Lisa, it's Officer Teller. It's okay. You're in no danger or trouble."

A tiny face emerged from behind a tree through a surrounding cloud of snowflakes.

A long breath—a sigh of relief—escaped Lucy without her being aware. "Come out. It's okay, Lisa. I just want to talk with you."

Lisa walked slowly from the tree, watching Lucy carefully. Lucy restrained herself from offering to hug the girl; she knew the sort of troubles Lisa had suffered from in the past—

neglected by her addict mother, abused by her teacher, Mr. Reilly, championed by Scott Brandt, and then stricken with grief at his death. She knew that, even if the little girl recognized her, Lisa would not respond readily to physical overtures. Lucy tried a safe smile, showing no teeth.

"What are you doing out on such a snowy morning, Lisa?"

"I came here to ask Scott to help me find my brother."

Now it was Lucy's turn to take a step back. A million questions flooded her mind. When she first met Lisa, she had immediately identified the symptoms of fetal alcohol syndrome: the thin lips, small stature, and withered arms. It was hard to tell how developmentally delayed Lisa was or even how old. Her small stature made her look younger than she probably was. If Lucy had to guess, she'd say ten, but she was sure that she was mentally and emotionally younger. Lucy had to sort out her questions and ask them one at a time, taking care not to overwhelm Lisa.

"I didn't know you had a brother," Lucy said, trying to sound cheerful. "How old is he?"

"Don't know. He hasn't had a birthday yet."

That took care of Lucy's next question; she didn't have to bother asking whether he had just wandered off somewhere. "How were you hoping Scott could help you?"

"I'm not sure, but I know he's the only one who's ever been able to help me. I guess he did it by bringing you. Did he bring you?"

Lucy wondered. Perhaps it was the magical thinking of a little girl, or maybe she was making a connection neither of them fully understood.

"When is the last time you saw your brother?"

"Last night I woke up and saw a witch pick him up and swallow him through a hole in the back of his neck."

This time, Lucy not only stepped back, but she was sure she blinked once or twice too. She didn't even know what to ask next. She had heard about witches since she was a little girl. Witches were alive and well on the rez, at least as far as rumors were concerned. But they were more likely to be talked about by the elders, the people to whom Lucy referred as aunt and uncle, even though there was often no blood relation. Lucy was not as likely to hear it from younger people, especially ones who interacted regularly with white people. This, like so much else of their tradition, continued to be lost.

"Besides the fact that he swallowed your brother through a hole in the back of his neck, is there another reason you thought he was a witch?"

Lisa began to get excited and to speak rapidly. "Yes, he had square feet, a third eye in the middle of his forehead, and he had a painted face. Then he told me when he saw I was awake that he'd make my mother and me sick if I woke my mother or called the police. He must have put a spell on my mother because I can't wake her up. He was big and strong but he looked like he was about a hundred years old."

"Did your brother cry when the man picked him up?"

"No, my brother doesn't cry much. He mostly just lies in his crib. When I try to pick him up or play with him, Mama tells me to let him alone, because he's happiest when he's by himself."

"What season was it when your mother had the baby?"

"It was early spring. I know, because the days were getting longer, more light was out, and the snow was almost gone, but there weren't any leaves on the trees yet."

Lucy calculated that the baby would be about nine months old, too old to be just lying in his crib. Maybe that was just the mother's way of not letting Lisa pick him up. Lucy's head was spinning. There were so many questions. "What did you do after the man left?"

"I tried to wake my mother, but I couldn't. She's been taking more of her cooking medicine lately, and it's hard to wake her, but I'm sure the witch did something. Then I went to the window to see where the man-witch had gone, but it was snowing so hard I couldn't see. I went back to bed and talked with Scott. I asked him to help me. At school, he liked it when I brought him flowers, so I tried to gather some to bring him, but mostly all I found were sticks. He always said he liked the sticks too."

"What is your mother doing now?"

"She's still sleeping. I couldn't wake her."

"How about if we both go over and give it a try?"

Lisa hesitated and stood frozen in place.

"Scott sent me to help you, Lisa. Please let me help." Lucy had said the magic word: "Scott." Lisa still looked hesitant, but Lucy could see her softening.

"Okay," she said, then a soft smile of relief spread over her face.

Lucy wondered about the power Scott must have had to make such an impression on these kids in such a short time. She felt a wave of sadness flood over her—sadness that such a force for good had been removed so prematurely from the world. As she thought of him, she remembered once again the look of despair and defeat in Scott's father's eyes at the loss of his son's powerful life. She would always remember it.

She dismissed the thought to concentrate again on the business at hand. "Come on, Lisa," she said. "Let's go over to your house."

Lucy and Lisa got into the squad car and drove a short way down Bear Trap Falls Road, past the intersection of 55 and farther and farther away from the accident site. Lucy noticed how frequently Lisa looked back behind them.

Lucy had been in Lisa's house once before, when she had asked the mother to allow Lisa to speak with the child psychologist at the tribal clinic. The mother had given permission readily enough; she hadn't been sober enough to do anything else.

Now, entering the house again, Lucy felt a shiver run down her spine. It was like reentering her own past life. The house was small like most houses on the rez; once inside, she could see everything but the two bedrooms, which were down a short hallway. Lisa's mother was lying on the couch. This time it wasn't just alcohol. One arm dangled down to the floor, and Lucy could immediately see the tracks of regular intravenous heroin injections. There were old scars running the length of her left arm, standing out light and scraggly against the woman's dark skin. Scattered randomly in these old track marks were fresh-scabbed injection sites. It reminded Lucy of the white lines down the middle of a road. It was a good analogy; mainlining drugs was like taking the road to self-destruction. Loved ones were cast aside or destroyed along the way. It was like car wrecks piled up along the side of the highway. Lucy felt sick at the thought of her own past; of her own car wrecks, and wrecks that might have been.

As she approached the woman, Lucy could tell she was barely breathing, and when she took her pulse, it was faint and slow. She was looking at a face that reminded her of her own, reflected in a mirror five years earlier. It was a mixture of old and young: there were few wrinkles, which gave the impression of a young face, but the puffiness and lack of care made her look old beyond her years.

Lucy reached without delay for the radio attached to her belt. "Send an ambulance immediately to Bear Trap Falls Road. Tell the paramedics to bring a dose of Narcan. We'll also need a crime scene investigation. There is a little boy, approximately nine months old, missing and possibly abducted. I don't know the address, but it's just off 55. My squad car is right outside in front of the house and I'll turn on my lights."

Lucy ran out to her squad and turned the dome lights back on. When she turned around, Lisa, about whom she had almost forgotten, was right behind her looking pale and panic-stricken.

"What's the matter with my mommy, and what are you doing?"

Lucy started to reach for her and then remembered the reaction when she had done that once before. She also remembered how Lisa referred to the heroin. She kept her distance. "Your mommy has taken too much of her medicine, and that's why you can't wake her up. I called some people to give her an antidote that will make her feel better."

"What's an auntie-dote, and will they take me away from her?" Lisa's eyes were as big as saucers.

It was surreal, reminiscent of when she and Lisa had a similar conversation once before. Then she had promised Lisa that she wasn't trying to take her away from her mother. Now she didn't know how things would turn out. She answered Lisa's first question.

"It's another kind of medicine that will make her feel better real fast. You'll see. They may have to take your mother to a hospital for a while, but you can stay with me and my kids while she gets better." Lucy could see that her words were making no impact on Lisa. She could see her mind drift somewhere else, somewhere safe. Lucy knew in Lisa's world, perhaps the only safe place she had ever found had been taken from her. Scott had become a safety net for Lisa, and she missed him terribly.

Just cling to Scott, Lucy thought. Find something of Scott to cling to.

With the falling snow, the ambulance was slow to arrive, but, once there, the paramedics quickly assessed the situation and gave Lisa's mother an injection of Narcan. Within seconds, her eyes opened, and she was able to speak. Her first question was, "Where's Lisa?" and her eyes darted nervously around the room.

Lucy was amazed about two things: first was how quickly the Narcan worked, and second, that the mother didn't say, "Where are my children?" just, "Where's Lisa?"

In that brief moment, Lucy remembered something she had read in the early days of recovery. For all the pain and suffering that heroin had caused, it was at least indirectly responsible for the major scientific discovery of receptor sites on the nervous system—places at the end of the nerves where tiny little chemical messengers help the nerves to communicate with each other and with the brain.

When former president Richard Nixon declared his war on crime, his advisors told him one of the quickest ways of reducing crime was to win the war on drugs. Users trying to support their habit are responsible for a large number of burglaries, robberies, murders, and prostitution—to name just a few crimes. The Nixon administration began to sink large amounts of money into research on causes of drug abuse. It was then that the use of methadone as an alternative to heroin was put into practice. Methadone is no less serious a drug than heroin, but because methadone is legal, it can be administered to addicts in a clinical setting. With methadone, addicts can take a drug at safe levels and at no cost and know what they are getting. This means they do not have to commit crimes to support their habit. It also puts them in contact with drug counselors who can help them get their lives back together. Other related research led to the discovery of receptor sites on the nerves, which respond to the body's own natural opiates called endorphins. Endorphins are released in response to pain and pleasure. They play a major role in such things as a runner's high and the reduction of pain. Endorphins are secreted at higher levels during sex and even laughter. Heroin is structurally very similar to endorphins and that is why it works so well in the human body. Narcan is one medication used to inactivate the effects of heroin; it fits into the nerve's receptor sites (similar to a key in a lock) even better than heroin, and replaces the heroin on these sites, but in all others ways Narcan is an inert drug. Narcan even replaces endorphins.

When the paramedics gave the drug to Lisa's mother, Lucy watched the girl's reaction too. Lisa's eyes opened wide. For the first time since losing her brother, Lisa saw something to give her hope, and maybe someone to believe in again. What Lucy said would happen—did happen. Lisa could not understand why this police lady was telling her the truth. Such a thing didn't often occur in Lisa's world.

Lucy began to question Lisa's mother and found out that her name was Dawn. There was a child, a baby boy. Dawn had awakened after Lisa had gone to find both of her children missing in the midst of a snowstorm. She spoke of her missing children without alarm, glancing vaguely toward Lisa, but not continuing to look for her son. Lucy could easily piece together several new facts. Faced again with her failure as a mother, Dawn had taken a larger than normal hit of heroin. Though the heroin wasn't directly affecting Dawn's nervous system at that moment, years of abuse still affected her brain. Lucy realized she would get very little relevant information from Dawn at present.

Lucy changed tactics and began trying to convince her to go to treatment. Dawn's first question was, "What will happen to my children?"

"Lisa could stay with me," said Lucy, "and at the moment, your son is missing." This seemed to hit Dawn for the first time, but all that registered on her face was a confused look.

"I don't need treatment," said Dawn doggedly.

Lucy looked her in the eye. "Dawn, look at me. You and I are both addicts. I have children too. At one point, mine were taken from me. You've already lost one child because you were too stoned to hear an intruder enter your house. The police are not going to believe your daughter's story, and right now, you will be the number one suspect in the disappearance of your son. If you don't want help for yourself, damn it, do it for your children."

Reluctantly, Dawn finally agreed, and the paramedics took her to the Maehnowesekiyah treatment center just outside Keshena.

Lucy decided she and Lisa would just be in the way. Investigators would be arriving soon, right after the ambulance left. When they did arrive, Lucy answered their questions and asked if she could be of any help. They suggested that the most helpful thing would be to remove Lisa from the home. It was the answer Lucy expected and hoped for. They had asked Lisa the same questions that Lucy had with the same results. They examined the pathway Lisa said the intruder had taken on his departure, but the snow had covered any tracks that might have remained. Lisa did not know which way the car had gone. She wasn't even sure there was a car. Lucy drove home slowly and dropped Lisa off with her mother and children.

Lucy's mother said little when she brought the child in, but Lucy saw the look. She turned to her children and said, "We have to be nice to Lisa. Her mother is in the hospital, and her little brother is missing."

Then she turned to her mother and noticed that the expression on her face had changed. "I talked her mother into going to Maehnowesekiyah. I hope it helps her as much as it did me. I'll be home as soon as my shift is over to help you with dinner. Lisa can sleep in my room. I'll sleep on the couch. I sleep better there anyway."

Just for a moment, Lucy thought she saw a smile and a look of pride on her mother's face.

Lisa was watching Lucy closely, and looked uncomfortable —or even desperate—as she saw her protector returning to the squad car, and leaving her in a house full of strangers.

Lucy's daughter, Tara, stepped up and took Lisa by the hand. "I still have some dolls in my room that I've been saving. Maybe we could dress them up."

Lisa smiled. Now it was Lucy's turn to feel proud.

She went off to finish her shift, confident that all would be well for Lisa. At least, for a time.

At dinner that night, Lucy noticed the dynamics around the table had changed. Usually the kids fought, and Lucy and her mother would take turns refereeing and trying to change the subject to something more positive. That night, everyone seemed on their best behavior. The kids asked Lisa questions about her school and told her about theirs. Lisa, for her part, seemed sometimes to focus, while at others she seemed to drift away, perhaps to thoughts of her mother or brother or maybe even to Scott. She was missing them all. Without knowing why, she responded to the kindness around her and tried to keep a brave face. All the while, her little heart felt like it would burst.

Lucy watched her and prayed silently for herself and for the wounded child that had been placed so unexpectedly in her care. Great Spirit, she prayed, I could really use some help right now. Please help me to help her.

She repeated the prayer to herself throughout the evening. She was already exhausted and needed all the help she could get.

THE NEXT DAY, LUCY drove Lisa to school in her truck. She tried to engage the girl in conversation about school, but Lisa got that faraway look and said little. After dropping her off, Lucy drove to the tribal office of family services to speak to Karen Fish.

The very thought of Karen had once filled Lucy with terror and hatred. Karen was the woman who had taken Lucy's children from her. She was a powerful woman even without the authority of her position. Physically, she looked like many Menominee women. She wore her dark hair long and straight. She was about about five feet six inches tall. Her legs and hips were slender, but her upper body was large in comparison. She had broad shoulders, long arms, large breasts, and a stomach that stuck out nearly as far as her breasts.

Her face could look determined and firm or compassionate and kind depending on whether she was talking to a child, a judge, or an abusive or neglectful parent. She was a woman whose strong convictions and values were evident in every fiber of her being. She didn't sway from them, nor could anyone in her charge. If you were against her and her values, you had a formidable opponent. If you worked with her and she knew you loved your children, then you had a powerful advocate who would speak to anyone on your behalf.

In all things, Karen Fish was a passionate woman.

Lucy still shook with anticipation every time she went through the door of Karen's office. When Karen turned to her with her piercing eyes, Lucy felt as if every sin she had committed was revealed on her face. But Karen just smiled warmly and inquired, "How's my favorite police officer doing?"

Lucy managed to stutter out that she and her family were doing well. "I'm here to ask you if you ever had occasion to work with Dawn Lake and her daughter, Lisa. They live over on Bear Trap Falls Road." She added, feeling clumsy, "Oh, and she also has a son." As she stumbled over the addition, feeling all of its awkwardness, Lucy panicked internally. She hated not having her ducks in a row when she talked to Karen. She couldn't remember whether she had ever heard the boy's name or if she just couldn't remember it. When she looked up in embarrassment at Karen, she realized it didn't matter because Karen's mind was already someplace else.

"Michael," she said with a sad look on her face. "His name is Michael. I was this close to taking those children from her last week," Karen said, holding her thumb and index finger an inch apart. "Now you're going to tell me that something has happened to them, and I will have to add them to the list of things that will haunt me in my old age." Her keen eyes returned to Lucy's face. "That's why I can never retire."

Lucy was shocked. She realized for the first time that as hard as Karen could be on others for their mistakes, it was nothing compared to the expectations to which she held herself. For all the confidence that she displayed, Karen was not above second-guessing herself.

"Well, sometime either late Saturday night or early Sunday morning, Michael disappeared."

Karen's face registered so many different feelings that Lucy lost track, but she definitely saw confusion and regret.

Karen spoke to the confusion first. "That child was failure to thrive. There's no way he got up and walked away. What could have happened?"

"If you talk to Lisa, she will tell you that a witch with three eyes, square feet, and a painted face came in and swallowed the boy in one gulp through the mouth in the back of his neck, then disappeared into a snowstorm. What does 'failure to thrive' mean?"

"The boy is not developing the way he should, and there doesn't appear to be any medical reason for it. It usually happens due to a lack of stimulation, particularly tactile stimulation a baby gets from being held and cuddled. Children can actually die from it. A witch? Do you believe her?"

"I believe Lisa believes it happened. I think that Lisa had a dream that, to her, explained the disappearance of her brother. I convinced the mother to go into treatment. I really don't know this for sure, but I suspect she will be the number one suspect. Do you have any idea what she might be capable of doing?"

"If I would have thought she was actually capable of harming either of those children, they would have been out of there, so obviously I had my doubts. The problem is, where do you place children with failure to thrive syndrome and fetal alcohol syndrome? Of course, that also leads to the question: who would abduct children like that?" Karen gazed towards the ceiling.

It dawned on Lucy that she had never heard Karen use the term 'kid' or 'kids.' I bet she would say kids are baby goats, she thought. It spoke to the respect she had for children.

"Well, that is one reason I haven't totally discounted Lisa's story. I've heard of groups that use ki... children in sacrifices. Perhaps kidnapping a child like that would prompt less concern, and less heat. Maybe police don't look as hard, particularly when the mother is a drug addict. They probably figure she's really the one responsible for the disappearance."

"Oh, that's awful," said Karen with horror. "Why didn't I remove those children?" Lucy could see the deep regret in her eyes.

Lucy spoke in a firm voice. "Now don't be so hard on yourself. Remember, we don't know anything yet. Is there anything else you can tell me about this case that might give us a clue?"

"Like what?"

"Well, for instance is there a father out there? Might he be interested in Michael?"

Karen shook her head in disgust. "The father is also her supplier. He could be a suspect in the disappearance, but only if he found someone who'd pay him for Michael. I wouldn't even put it past him if he left Michael on a snowbank somewhere. He's like a man without a soul. But my guess is, if the baby were disturbing him in any way, he'd just leave. I think if there is any hope for Dawn, she needs to kick that guy to the curb, as the expression goes."

Lucy nodded soberly. "By the way," she said, "I took Lisa home with me last night. Is it okay if she stays with us for a while? I think she's doing my kids some good."

Karen smiled then. "You are one reason I could retire. I could sit by the river and watch it go by, and think of the families for whom I'd made a difference. Then cases like this one would come up, and I'd jump into the river. Yes, it's fine. I'll note it in her file."

"Don't give up hope. Maybe we will find Michael." Even as she said it, Lucy felt little hope herself. She had no idea where to turn. Perhaps the crime scene investigators had turned up something. She decided to walk back to the station. Lucy thought of her own two children as she walked. Suddenly, she was missing them both very much. They had recovered so much in recent months, but every day was a fresh challenge. She was always happy to have that feeling of missing her family and looking forward to seeing them all. She smiled to herself—she even felt a stirring for her mother.

chapter 3

THE STATION WAS WITHIN walking distance of Karen's office, so Lucy had parked there while she visited Family Services. The sky was now blue and the snow had moved east, probably to somewhere over Detroit by now. The temperature had dropped but not severely and the high-pressure system must have moved quickly because the winds were calm. The area was blanketed in white and it looked beautiful. Lucy wished she could get out in the middle of the woods and appreciate the peace that the snow provided. She was even tempted to drive through it, but the snow was so deep she didn't trust her truck off road.

On her way into the station, she met Ray Waupuse. A smile spread across his face as soon as he saw her and Lucy's face mirrored his.

"I hear you're involved in a new mystery now. Don't you think you should retire while you're batting a thousand?" he asked with a smile and a wink.

"Do you still believe in those patron saints they used to teach us about in the mission school? Wasn't there one for hopeless causes? Maybe you could pray to that guy for me."

"Which is the hopeless cause that I should pray for? You or the one you are investigating?"

Lucy wrinkled her nose and gave him a disapproving look she didn't mean.

"I'm sure if I leave this new one to the department or the FBI, they are going to pin it on the mother, and she's got enough to worry about right now. Even if she is responsible, I'd like her to think that someone is on her side. I don't think she has anyone." Lucy added to herself that she remembered what that was like.

Ray shook his head. "I worry about you. I think you may just be too kind to be a cop."

Lucy smiled. "I need to be mean and heartless like you are, right?"

Now it was Ray's turn to give a disapproving look he didn't mean. "I talked to your supervisor. Maybe for this case, you can at least use department time instead of your own. I knew you'd want to pursue it. I also organized a group of my friends to search the area with snowmobiles this afternoon if you want to join us."

Lucy smiled and gently touched Ray's arm. "I was just going to talk with him about that. Thanks for running interference. Now that Lisa is living with us, I can't afford to leave my mother with my kids and Lisa too while I pretend to be a detective."

"I'm not sure I've done you any favors," Ray said ruefully. "I talked to one of the investigators, and they found nothing that would indicate any kind of intruder. You know as well as I do, these cases almost always end up being a parent who gets angry and goes too far, then covers it up with an intruder story."

"In this case, though, it's not the mother saying that, it's the sister."

"Maybe the sister was playing with him too rough?" Ray asked in a confrontational tone.

"In the middle of the night? And besides, would she be smart enough to come up with the kind of story that she did to cover her own tracks? Lisa wouldn't be able to come up with that story. I'm convinced that she saw what she described. It may have been in a dream, but she didn't make up seeing it."

"Well, all you need to do then is find a witch with three eyes, square feet, and a very large mouth in the back of his neck. That should be easy," Ray said with an endearing sideways smile.

Lucy was surprised he knew so much detail. "Boy, word sure does travel around here, doesn't it?"

"I'm convinced that if it has anything to do with witches, everybody knows about it in just a few hours. We're like kids during Halloween all year round."

"I guess so. Well, thanks for your help with my supervisor. Also promise me you'll let me know if you see the witch... I mean, the person you just described."

"I'll be sure to do that. You take care of yourself, Lucy."

"I will."

Then, just like always, Ray walked away, and Lucy felt disappointed. She felt like she was missing something. What was she looking for that she didn't get? She asked herself this question, as she always did, but no answer came.

Lucy took a deep breath and went in to see her supervisor. It wasn't that Lucy didn't like her supervisor or that he didn't like her or that she thought he didn't like her; it was just that she seemed caught in a vicious cycle: every time she saw him, she did something stupid. This made her feel self-conscious whenever she saw him. And that increased the likelihood that she would do something stupid. And usually, sure enough, she did.

Lieutenant Moon was sitting behind his desk when Lucy walked into his office. The desk was large and that added to Lucy's feeling of intimidation. He was a big man and that didn't help either. He was taller than most Menominee and had a large barrel chest and stomach. His hair was black, as were his eyes. He wore reading glasses and would always peer over them at Lucy, intensifying her feeling of being judged.

In her mind, she imagined he was already cringing inside at the thought of her presenting him with another harebrained scheme or theory. Back when she was working on the Brandt case he would frequently ask her about any new developments that he could take to the FBI, adding that he knew she was pursuing the case on her own. She always had to answer no. Then he'd look over his glasses at her and ask again: "Nothing?" She would then speak for him, and say that she knew he thought she should give it up, but she wasn't ready to do that yet. He wouldn't say anything and then she'd wonder to herself why she had assumed so much, and the cycle would continue.

This time, Lucy started talking from the moment she walked into the room. She decided to take a different tack. "I know it's not part of my job description, sir," she said, "but I'd like to try to help Lisa and her mom."

"So you believe the little girl's story," Lieutenant Moon said, looking over his glasses.

"I don't know about that," Lucy said quickly. "I just think, as a good detective, you should leave all of your options open."

"So you've promoted yourself to detective now, Officer Teller?" Lieutenant Moon asked. There was a hint of a smile on his face.

"No, it's not that. It's just that I was hoping you'd let me pursue this case, especially since none of us seem to have a clue what's going on here."

"So you're assuming the crime scene investigators found nothing?"

"Well, not that, sir. Well, yes, I guess I did assume that." She could feel her face getting slightly flushed.

"They did find a trace of blood in the child's crib and some on the couch where the mother was lying, but admittedly not enough to assume foul play." For the first time Lucy could remember, Lieutenant Moon actually smiled. She got the impression that maybe he enjoyed seeing her flustered. "We don't know much about this case, and I think you're the best officer we have to pursue it, given your background. You can take half of your time to investigate. Just keep track of your hours, and keep me abreast of what you find," he finished, and leaned back in his chair.

"Thank you, sir. I'll need your advice. This is pretty new to me."

"You need to start by organizing a search party. I'll help you with that part." Then came the most astonishing moment of this unusual interview. Locking eyes with Lucy, Lieutenant Moon said, "I'm glad it was you who found the little girl." Then he dismissed her.

For a change, Lucy walked out of Lieutenant Moon's office feeling better than when she went into it. Unfortunately, the good feeling lasted only a short time. When she read the report from the crime scene investigators, she realized that she had nothing to go on; nothing that didn't point to Dawn getting rid of her son. There had to be more. There just had to be more information.

What was she missing?

chapter 4

Lucy went to visit Dawn the next day at the treatment center. She was reminded of the dark heaviness she had felt as she went into treatment. Like most people, she had entered feeling dirty.

Dawn would still be detoxing and probably would be able to provide little information, but Lucy wanted to show her support. She knew this would be a crucial time, and that support might help to keep Dawn in treatment. Her body would be screaming for drugs and she would be begging to leave treatment—Lucy remembered those feelings clearly. The memory of her horrific struggle to get clean was one of the things that helped to keep her sober every day.

Lucy stopped first to visit Dr. Meany. Meany wasn't his real name; it was Wolf, but in detox, everyone is in pain—physical, emotional, and spiritual pain. The medical doctor is in charge of dispensing drugs to help ease the pain, but no matter how much he dispenses, it's less than the patients are used to getting from their own self-medication. Patients always wanted more than Dr. Wolf was willing to provide. Hence the patients' nickname for him: Dr. Meany.

He really didn't deserve the name. His compassion for addicts was well-founded in personal experience. Many years before, Dr. Wolf had ignored the pressures of the rez in order to do well in school and left its familiarity for the first time to attend college. Alone and afraid in a strange world, he struggled through college and got into medical school.

There, he had felt an emptiness that was hard to describe. He could not understand it himself. He desperately missed the familiarity of his people and the ways of the reservation. All the while, he avoided the alcohol that had gotten so many of his family members in trouble. He finished medical school and went into residency for neurosurgery. He was well on his way to completing it, when he made what seemed to him a brilliant discovery. He could help relieve all the pressures—of residency and working extra jobs and paying off student loans—simply by prescribing medication for himself.

As he talked about it later in meetings, he noted how hard it was to believe that a medical student wouldn't realize that by taking minor tranquilizers he was just eating booze, but it didn't register. He had avoided the lure of alcohol and considered he had done very well for himself.

Soon he became hopelessly addicted. A DUI helped him to come to his senses before he destroyed his life and his medical career and his stint in treatment changed his focus from neurosurgery to addictionology. When he had finished his residency at the Betty Ford Clinic, he had come back to Keshena, where he'd been for ten years.

What he was unwilling to dispense in medication, Dr. Meany gave instead in endless hours of time and the willingness to care, to understand, and to be available through the hard times. For all of this, he was rewarded with endless anger and criticism.

Lucy was, at first, convinced that Meany was a quack. She thought he had a lot of nerve for someone who didn't know half of what she knew about drugs. But eventually Lucy came to value all he had done for her. She was willing to admit that, when it came to drugs, all she knew was getting herself in trouble, and that it was time to trust somebody else. That someone was Dr. Meany and the team at Maehnowesekiyah. They saved her life and gave her kids back their mother.

Now, she tried never to let an opportunity pass to atone for all the abuse she had given the doctor in those first few weeks. She was eternally grateful and had a deep respect for him. When she stopped at his office, he wasn't there. She asked at the nurses' station where Dawn Lake's room was, and if she could visit. The nurse was friendly and recognized Lucy as a regular volunteer. She told her the room number.

"The doctor is down there now and probably could use some reinforcements," the nurse added, as she smiled and rolled her eyes toward the ceiling.

As Lucy walked down the hall, she could hear Dawn using a variety of rhetorical tactics to persuade Dr. Wolf to increase her meds. She ranged between semi-seductive to whining to questioning his skills as a physician. Dr. Wolf's response was always the same: "I understand you're in pain and not sleeping well. All of that is your body's response to learning to live without heroin and alcohol. I'm giving you as much medication as I can responsibly give you. Part of your recovery is learning to trust and giving control of your drug use over to someone other than yourself. You can help yourself by beginning to go to group therapy and learning to connect with people again. Try to get out of yourself and the pain you are in and focus on others. It is about time you got out of yourself and started looking outside of this disease."

Dawn was getting frustrated and anger came next. "I don't need no damn group. I need rest. I need to stop being in pain. I thought this place was supposed to help you, not hurt you. Since I've been here, all I do is get worse. I can't stand the way I'm feeling." Then, with the rapidity of a desperate addict, she switched again. "You've got to help me," she pleaded. She began to cry with gut-wrenching sobs.

Dr. Wolf continued with the same soft and kind approach. "If you had a malignant tumor and went in to have it removed, you might go into the hospital pain free, but after the surgery was performed, you'd probably hurt like hell. The same is true here. Sometimes you have to feel worse before you feel better, but if you stick with us for a while, you're going to feel better than you have in years. You've got to trust me," he said in a firm, fatherly voice.

Lucy knocked softly on the door. "You still using those same tired lines, Doc?" she asked as she leaned in.

He turned slightly toward her to smile a welcome, but did not turn fully away from Dawn.

Lucy walked in slowly and gave the doctor an encouraging pat on his shoulder, but did it so it was out of Dawn's view. Since Dawn was already mad at him, Lucy didn't want to be guilty by association. Of course, since she was the one who had talked her into coming here, she probably already was.

"I know it feels like they aren't doing enough for you," she said to Dawn, "and I don't blame you for feeling that way, but I was where you are several years ago. These people saved my life and gave my kids their mother back. You need to trust them."

"What are you doing here?" Dawn spat out in response. "Why aren't you out looking for my boy?"

"I have a group of snowmobilers mobilized to begin searching for him this afternoon. I came here to ask you some questions that might help in our search, and to tell you we'll do all we can to find your son."

Sneering, Dawn turned to Dr. Wolf. "See? Besides all the physical pain that I'm in, I have a son out there lost in the snow. I need something to help me sleep."

"Just like you have to learn to cope with physical pain without drugs, you need to learn to cope with emotional pain without them," he answered with the same calm patience.

"Is there anything you thought of since I last talked with you," Lucy persisted, "anything that might help us to find your son?"

"I thought that was your job. Just find him." Dawn's eyes sparked and fired shooting darts of anger at both Lucy and the doctor.

Lucy marveled at Dr. Wolf's patience. She had been there for only a few minutes and already she wanted to wring Dawn's neck. "Dr. Wolf can help you get better, but if it really happens, it'll eventually be up to you. I can help find your son, but if you want him found, you have to do your part, too. That's another reason you need to go to group; the other patients won't put up with your crap the way he does. Quit biting the hands that are trying to feed you."

If Dawn heard any of it, she gave no indication. "I need to rest now." Dismissing them from her room, Dawn went to her bed and began gently rocking with her arms wrapped around her legs, and knees tucked under her chin.

Dr. Wolf motioned with his head for Lucy to follow him into the hall. As they walked down the hall, Lucy asked, "What do you think, Doc?"

"She's got to be willing to trust and to let other people inside."

"I think it's going to be difficult for her to trust if we don't find some way of verifying that there was an intruder in her house who took her son. Then if something has happened to her son, she'll have to deal with the grief and anger and guilt of his loss. She is in a tough situation, but she needs the truth, and that will complicate her recovery as well. No matter what the case, you'll have a challenge on your hands with this one."

"No worse than you were," Doc said with a smile and a quick wink.

"That's true. If you could get through to me, you can get through to anyone," Lucy said, grabbing his arm as they continued down the hall.

"I don't know about that, but I'm glad you and others like you come back to remind us that we are successful sometimes. Now," he said, detaching her gently from his arm, "go and do your job and let us do ours."

She was dismissed. Lucy was dismissed for a third time that day.

chapter 5

As she turned her snowmobile up another trail, Lucy began to think she knew what snow blindness was like. Everywhere she looked, she saw white. With all the new snow, there was no real evidence to be found anywhere. There were no footprints, no bloodstains, and—luckily—no tiny bodies anywhere in the snow. As darkness closed in, she gathered with the other searchers, and they each reported the same. They saw nothing.

The next day, they tried snowshoes so they could get off the trails, but disappointingly, still found nothing. Lucy did come across a hiking trail that she didn't know existed and it appeared that someone had been on it at some point either before or during the storm, but she found nothing on it that would indicate the kidnapper might have gone that way. The trail was narrow and cut in such a way to discourage any snowmobilers from traveling on it. Not only that, occasionally a large tree stood in the middle of the trail, and the tracks went to one side or the other. Lucy stopped and looked around frequently for anything that might be remotely helpful.

She saw nothing, but on occasion, she did appreciate that seeing nothing meant there was no evidence of foul play. She found herself, instead, savoring the beauty. The woods were completely quiet. She saw evidence of deer tracks in the snow. The small thin saplings, that had to grow up rapidly to fight with the taller trees for the sun, would bend over under the weight of the snow and touch the ground. They created arches of white that reminded her of the arches brides walked under in magazine ads. Her mind drifted to her own life. She wondered if there would ever be a man in her life again. In her marriage, she and her husband had been much more married to drugs than to each other. Drugs finally killed him and would probably have killed her if Karen hadn't intervened.

Her life since had been filled with recovery, her children, her job, and recently some courses at the College of Menominee Nation. It was a full life, but as she learned about real closeness with others, she began to think it might be interesting to be in a relationship again that could be a barometer for how far she had come.

As if answering her thought, she heard Ray's voice softly behind her. "We'd better start heading back. It will be dark soon, and we move a lot slower on these snowshoes."

"You startled me," she said. "How long have you been following me?" Lucy knew her reaction was more than just surprise. She felt her face flush. Butterflies were fluttering in her stomach, and she barely stopped herself from giggling.

"I've been about a hundred yards to your right and slightly behind you for a while now. You know I walk in these woods a lot. I drive a four-wheeler during the summer and hunting season, and I never came across this trail before. It must be new. I wonder who built it and where it leads." He gently put his arm around her shoulder in a safe brotherly way. Lucy leaned into him briefly.

"I don't know," said Lucy, "but I was wondering the same thing. Still, is there any reason to believe it has anything to do with Michael's disappearance? We've been searching these woods for two days now, and for all we know, the kidnapper might have left in a car. Come to think of it, we don't even know if there was such a person."

They turned and headed back to Dawn's house to meet up with the rest of the search party.

"Well," said Ray, "we do know that there is a child and that he is missing. He has to be somewhere. We know that there is probably not going to be a ransom demand, because Dawn has no money. It could be someone to whom she owed money, but still, how do you get blood from a turnip? We have to hope that this person wanted to keep the child alive, but why this child? I'm sorry, but the most logical explanation is the mother or her boyfriend lost their temper and that they disposed of the child somewhere."

Ray and Lucy stood in silence for a time, feeling a sick tightness in their stomachs. Then Ray spoke again. "Why don't you let me talk to the boyfriend tomorrow to see what his story is?"

"I'd appreciate that, but this is three days you're spending on this case. You sure you're not going soft on me?" Lucy tilted her head and smiled with her eyes.

Ray smiled back. "You need a lot of help. Since I know you're not going to leave this alone, I might as well do what I can. What is your next move?"

"I don't have one. I thought after the kids get out of school tomorrow, I'd take them up to see the Brandts. It would give my mother a break that I think she'd appreciate. Maybe she could even go to the casino and play some bingo with her buddies. I'd like to see how the Brandts are doing. I'm hoping that getting away from this for a while will give me some new ideas."

Lucy didn't know how true that might be. She didn't know what was coming her way.

chapter 6

WHEN THE CHILDREN came home from school, Lucy took the three of them on the hour-long drive to the Brandts' house. Her two would normally have fought most of the way, but with Lisa between them, they took turns entertaining her and listening to music instead of bickering.

They pulled up in front of the Brandt house and for a moment Lucy worried she might have taken the trip for nothing: there was nobody home. The children were getting tired of being in the car and she wasn't sure if she could convince them to wait long. Just as she was getting ready for the ride back, Hank Brandt slid across his lawn on cross-country skis. Lucy thought his face looked more relaxed than when she had last seen him. Certainly, when he saw her, his face brightened considerably.

Using his poles, he loosened the bindings on his skis and moved quickly to open the front door. She introduced her children to him, and Hank immediately made them feel welcome with cups of steaming hot chocolate. Lisa was very quiet. To Lucy's mind, the little girl seemed to want to hide behind her and avoid Hank at all costs. Lucy thought it might help to tell her that this was Scott's father, but it had little impact. Lisa had never met Hank, because she never had to testify at Mr. Reilly's trial. Reilly's exploitation of children did not even come up in the trial. Reilly was tried on his abduction of Lucy, threats against her life, and his confessed complicity in Scott's murder. Hank had attended the entire trial and the other family members came when they could. They did it as much to support Lucy as to look for justice. They didn't believe that bringing the killers to justice would do much for their healing, only that it would serve to keep these brutal men from hurting others.

One by one, the rest of the family trickled in. Lisa seemed to warm to Molly, Bobbie, Paul, and Sally, but not to Hank, hard as he tried. Lucy began to wonder what kind of relationship Lisa might have with Dawn's boyfriend. Why was the little girl afraid of this gentle man?

The Brandts' home seemed much less somber than her last visit and the kidding and laughter were pleasant for Lucy to see.

When they left, Lisa was quiet for the beginning of the ride, but Jerrod and Tara made plenty of noise to make up for it. When Lisa spoke, it was very softly and Lucy almost missed it.

"He had witch's feet," was all she said.

Lucy slowed the car and made a U-turn. Her heart was pounding, and she was more excited than she had been in a long time. Within minutes, they were back in the Brandts' driveway. When he answered the door, Hank had changed from his cross-country gear to jeans and a flannel shirt. Lucy apologized for the interruption and told Hank what Lisa had said. Hank was confused at first until Lucy told him about the description that Lisa had given her of the intruder. Hank immediately excused himself and returned with his ski boots. They were an old pair, the kind with a solid rubber square front with three holes in the bottom of each to fit on three pins sticking up from the ski.

Lisa's discomfort intensified when she saw the skis. She hid behind Lucy and, when urged to come out, only shook her head and whispered, "No, no. He's a witch."

Lucy assured Lisa that Hank was not a witch.

Lisa did not respond directly, but when she saw that the shoes came off, she was less afraid. Lucy began to think of the trail that she and Ray were on earlier. Maybe it was important. Now Hank was excited, and for a particular reason. Part of his recovery from alcoholism had come from nature. He loved it and participated in sports and activities every season. Molly and the kids were constantly teasing him about his gear. They never ran out of Christmas and birthday gifts to get him because he always wanted more. He kayaked, canoed, and biked in the summer. He and Molly had even gotten a tandem bicycle and and rode it on trails throughout Wisconsin. In the winter, he loved cross-country skiing and even did downhill because the kids liked that better.

"A witch and a hole in the back of his neck, square feet, a third eye, and a painted face." Hank repeated the description over and over. Lucy could almost see the wheels turning in his brain. He hurried from the room and returned a few moments later with his arms full of gear.

"You said it was most likely dark when the abduction took place, and that it was snowing?"

"Yes," Lucy answered.

They asked Lisa if she was aware of the time, but all she could say was that it was dark and she had been sleeping.

Hank pulled out a small flashlight with straps that he attached over his head. He positioned it so the small flashlight was facing out from the middle of his forehead. Lisa jumped back.

"Is that how the man looked?" Lucy asked her.

"Sort of," Lisa said. "But the eye was in his forehead."

Hank took a stocking cap from his pile, went to the kitchen, and got a pair of scissors. He cut a slit in the cap and pulled it over his head so that the lens of the light came through the slit.

Lisa grabbed Lucy's arm. "But it had an eye." She looked very confused and kept moving behind Lucy.

Hank called his daughter, Sally. Sally was becoming quite an artist and had paint supplies in the house. She painted an eye on the lens of the flashlight. Hank then reached up and twisted the light. It not only looked like an eye; it cast a strange shadow around the room.

"Creepy," said Lucy's daughter, Tara, speaking for the first time. She and Jerrod had been totally dumbfounded prior to this. They thought it was funny to watch the adults playing such a game.

"If he were skiing through the woods, he would have needed his hands free for the poles. Also, if the house was dark, this would have been great for seeing where he was going, without turning on any lights," Lucy whispered, not wanting to startle Lisa. She turned then to the girl. "He must have known your mother would be taking her medicine, and you'd be the only one who could tell. If you described something strange, no one would believe you. This getup is strange enough by itself, but he made it stranger in order to scare you and make him look like a witch." Lucy turned to Hank. "But what about swallowing the baby through a hole in the back of his neck?"

"Yeah, what about that, Dad?" Paul, Bobbie, and Sally asked in unison.

"Yeah, what about that, Hank?" Molly asked.

Now they had everyone's interest.

Hank told Sally to get one of the old dolls she kept in her bedroom. Meanwhile, he reached once more into his pile and pulled out a frame backpack. He stuck his hands and arms through the straps so the bag stood open on his back like a large box on its side, with the opening by his shoulders and facing up. He then put on a large coat several sizes too big to accommodate the backpack.

"I sometimes go to the grocery store on my skis. If it's cold and I don't want something to freeze, I do this. He wouldn't have wanted to take the time to dress the baby."

Sally came with a doll, and Hank took it, moved the collar backward, and put the doll inside the backpack.

"Swallowed the baby through a mouth in the back of his neck," they all said in unison.

"This is crude, of course," said Hank, "but if I had time to fix it up, I could make a comfortable compartment for a baby. I could also put diapers and bottles in the side compartments. I could even put a little hand warmer in there to keep the baby warm, and a breathing tube to bring in plenty of oxygen."

All eyes turned toward Lisa. She still stood shaking behind Lucy with tears in her eyes. "That's what I saw. I thought it was a witch that came to steal my baby brother."

Hank, coming out of the haze of his excitement and realizing how frightened the little girl had become, took off the outfit as quickly as he could.

"Lisa," Lucy asked, "is it okay to hug you?"

Lisa just nodded her head.

Lucy knelt down slowly and gave her a long hug. "I know that was scary for you, but now we understand what you were describing. We also know it wasn't a witch. Just like Mr. Brandt, it was someone pretending to be a witch. This will really help us to find your brother. You are a good helper, Lisa."

What Lucy didn't say was that for the first time she had hope that the boy might be alive and that neither Lisa's mother nor her boyfriend was guilty of murder. Anyone who went to this much trouble wasn't about to kill the child, at least not right away. She wondered how much time they had. With such a big lead, could they ever catch him?

"So when do we start going after this guy?" Hank asked, as he stood up quickly.

"We?" Lucy asked, with a hint of a smile and no sarcasm.

"I can start in the morning. It's winter. The construction company is closed for a couple of months, and you need lessons in skiing. Besides, I've lost a child. Nothing would give me more joy than helping to find one. I know what it's like to want desperately to fill the void of a missing child."

"Just because we now know this guy isn't a witch, doesn't mean he isn't dangerous. I can't ask you to risk your life for this."

"You're not asking." Hank was firm. "I'm volunteering."

"Hank, don't you think you and I should talk about this?" Molly spoke quickly and quietly. "Don't you think this family has suffered enough? What if something happens to you? How do you think we're going to feel?" She was only starting with her questions. The Brandt children were clustering around too, ready with their own questions.

Hank turned toward all of them. "You guys have to let me do this. You are all busy now with school, work, and friends. All I have is time to think, and I don't need that. I feel like I have a sense of this guy, and I don't think he's dangerous. He went to too much trouble to protect everyone."

"That doesn't tell us what he'd do if we cornered him," Lucy replied.

"I don't want to apprehend him. That's your job. I just want to help you find him and the baby." Hank's voice and eyes were pleading.

"I'd like to help, too," said Bobbie. "Since I'm not going back to school at the moment." Then, all of a sudden, she realized what she had said. There was guilt in her eyes and shame in her voice. "I dropped my classes," she explained quietly, then paused. "I just couldn't get motivated or concentrate. Failing would be too easy right now. I talked to Tom about it, but I guess I hadn't gotten up the courage to tell you. This would do me good too. I need to do something to make me feel better."

"Oh great, let me lose two more family members," Molly said sarcastically, throwing up her hands. She had tears in her eyes.

Hank put his arms around Bobbie and his wife. "We'll be back, and we'll have something to celebrate too."

Molly rolled her eyes, then sighed, suddenly deflated.

Lucy was in a dilemma. She wasn't as optimistic as Hank, nor was she as certain that there wouldn't be trouble. But she also knew snowmobiles wouldn't work on the trail she had traveled down yesterday and Hank was the only person she knew who cross-country skied. Snowshoes were too slow. She took a deep breath and decided. "Okay, if you guys decide as a family that you want to help, I'll clear it with my boss, and we can head out the day after tomorrow."

She left soon after.

When Hank crawled into bed that night, he could hear Molly sniffling. He lay there quietly for a while, not knowing what to say. Finally, he spoke. "Molly, I know this is hard for you to understand, but all my life I've wondered about whether or not I have courage. I've never been in a war or in a situation where I had to put my life on the line for the good of someone else. I see an opportunity here to prove something to myself, and maybe Bobbie needs to do the same. If I walk away from this, I'll have failed, and I just can't take another failure right now."

"Hank, you show courage every day. Don't you think I know how hard it is for you to get up every day and go to work, to fight your addiction, to be a good father, to live with me— especially to live with me? You are all about courage. Perhaps it would take more courage not to do this thing, and stay home with your wife and family who need you."

"I understand what you're saying and appreciate your love and concern for me, but let's all sacrifice for the good of this child. I promise I will not try to be a hero and get myself killed. I know my limitations. I just want to help."

"You already have, Hank. Lucy didn't have a clue in this case until she came here today."

"Can I ask for your support in this? Will you make this your sacrifice?"

Molly sighed. She rolled over and kissed him. "Come home to me," she said.

"I'm just beginning to feel connected to you and to life again. I don't want to lose that."

Hank reached out for his wife. They made love with intensity, knowing it could be the last time. They were both praying silently that it wouldn't be.

chapter 7

LUCY NEEDED TO TALK
to several people, starting with Ray. She called the station and
asked to be patched through to his radio. First, she asked Ray
what he had learned from the boyfriend. She was hoping he
had valuable information to add to her new theory. She was
disappointed.

"It isn't much," he admitted. "But he skipped town. I
issued a warrant for his arrest and notified the police in other
reservations. I think we may have our man."

"I don't think so," Lucy said and then she related the events
that had unfolded at the Brandts.

"Damn," said Ray. "That guy's good. Maybe we should
offer him a job."

"Well, we kind of have."

Confused silence was all Lucy heard on the other end.

She hurried to explain. "He offered to take me down that
path we were on yesterday. We're going to go on cross-country
skis. You interested?"

"You know, I've always wanted to try that," he said. "How are we going to get equipment? And how do we dress?"

"Hank says to dress in layers. Wear a wool sweater if you have one. It insulates even when it's wet, and if you have any kind of underwear that wicks the perspiration away from your body, wear that. Wear a windbreaker on the outside. If it's waterproof and breathable, all the better. He said he'd bring food and gear for overnight, if we need it."

After her conversation with Ray, Lucy glanced over some maps. The reservation totaled about two hundred thirty thousand acres. Trees covered ninety-five percent of it and the reservation ran up against the Nicolet National Forest, which was several hundred thousand acres more. Their kidnapper could be anywhere in those woods. He could have a car on any of the highways that traveled through it. Lucy knew that if they got too far from a highway and a patrol car, their radios wouldn't work. As she stared at the map and calculated their chances, Lucy wondered what she was getting herself and her friends into.

Next, she talked to her supervisor. When she went into his office, she knew she was in more trouble than usual. Standing next to the Lieutenant's desk was a tall, slender man with glasses that shouted FBI. The look on his face was well past confident; he was cocky. He smirked as she entered the room.

Lucy tried not to grimace. So not only did she have to try to convince the Lieutenant that Lisa's story was beginning to make sense—even while he kept looking over his glasses at her—she had to try to ignore FBI Agent Scruggs who was beside himself with amusement. She began her story.

When she was finished, Scruggs didn't even bother to address her; he spoke directly to the Lieutenant. "Why don't you let the little officer here go on her witch hunt while my men and I engage in serious police work?"

Then she asked for time to cross-country ski through the woods taking another officer, Ray Waupuse, and two civilian non-Natives with her. This gave Agent Scruggs a good chuckle. Still, the Lieutenant was happy not to have to assign additional officers to find Dawn's boyfriend. That would be the FBI's job. They might have better luck, since there was a good chance he would have left for another reservation anyway.

Lucy left the room relatively unscathed, and almost relieved.

The next and biggest challenge was her mother. Luckily, the kids were on her side with this, but she had to convince them that they couldn't go with her.

Her mother was furious. "I put up with your playing Injun with short runs and smudging, but this is ridiculous. It's cold out there and dangerous. You know nothing about surviving in the woods in the summertime, much less the winter. You're crazy. And then you're going to trust some white man who probably knows less than you do about survival to lead you around. You're crazy."

"Mom, I promise the kids will be good and that Jerrod and Tara will help." Lucy turned to them and spoke in a threatening tone. "Won't you?"

"I don't have a problem with these kids. It's you I'm worried about, you dope," said Lucy's mom. "And you haven't heard a word I said, have you?"

Lucy just looked at her, confused. She was searching for the right words to convince her mom. "Hank knows what he's doing as far as skiing and camping are concerned and I have Ray to help me with the police part of it. I don't think this guy is a killer."

"Just because you got some explanations for some of the things he does, don't you convince yourself he's not a witch and has powers you don't understand, young lady."

"I promise I won't take him lightly," Lucy assured her, moving closer.

"You already are," her mother replied with fear in her eyes. "You were easier to deal with on drugs." Her words were not intended to be hurtful, but they stung Lucy all the same. She stepped back, recoiling at the pain. She shook it off. She had one more person to talk to.

Her final stop was at the treatment center. She told Dawn about the recent developments and what she was planning to do. Lucy became even less hopeful as she spoke to the lost boy's mother.

If Dawn heard any of it, she didn't respond to it. She was frustrated, rude, and very angry. "You need to find my boyfriend, and he needs to bring me a little something just to take the edge off. Then maybe I can survive in here."

Lucy tried to understand and to remember the time when she was just like Dawn—but it was hard. While Dawn remained warm and dry, Lucy would be cold and wet and exhausted trying to find Dawn's neglected son. It helped to know that no matter how uncomfortable the winter elements were, she'd be in less pain than Dawn was because Dawn's was physical, emotional, and spiritual.

"We'll do our best," was all Lucy said before leaving the room.

This time she dismissed Dawn.

chapter *8*

RAY AND LUCY MET
Hank and Bobbie at the Pine Hills Golf Course for breakfast
the next day. Pine Hills had been bought by the Mohican
Nation a number of years ago. They had added an extra nine
holes to the course and built a beautiful restaurant several years
ago. Hank encouraged all of them to eat a heavy breakfast.
Each of them had eggs and meat, and whole wheat pancakes
or toast.

Speaking from experience, Hank said, "Meals from here
on will be fast and not that exciting."

As they were eating, Hank went over with them what they
had brought for clothes. He was concerned that Lucy had jeans
and cotton long underwear. She did have a lightweight nylon
jacket, but it wasn't breathable. Both Lucy and Ray had layers
of clothing, but they found it hard to believe they'd be warm
enough. When he heard about the layers that Ray had planned
to wear, Hank convinced him to take a few off and put them
in his backpack.

"It's better to start off cold," he told them. "You can always add layers if you continue to be cold, but if you start to perspire, and your skin gets wet, it will be hard to warm up again. If your core temperature begins to drop, that's hypothermia and it can be fatal if we can't get it up again. I'm going to let you guys worry about the enemy we're chasing; my main enemy is winter. Winter can be just as deadly as anyone with a gun." He had brought Molly's Gortex pants and jacket for Lucy and some of Ryan's supplies for Ray.

When they had finished breakfast, they drove in two cars to Lisa's house. Hank took out skis, poles, and boots for everyone. He had a backpack filled with some of the food, clothes, and a sleeping bag. For Bobbie and for himself, as they were the experienced skiers, he had a sled he would pull behind him on the trail with a four-person tent and the remainder of the food. He gave smaller and lighter packs to Lucy and Ray for their clothes, personal items, and sleeping bags. After putting on their boots, Ray and Lucy got their first skiing lesson. Hank taught them how to put on the skis first, then he had them practice gliding without their poles.

"You want to press down and backwards when the ski is directly beneath you," Hank instructed them. Lucy was excited and relieved when both she and Ray picked this up quickly.

Next, Hank handed them poles. They put their hands through the straps first and then grabbed the poles on the grip with their thumbs over the straps. "Many people use the poles just to help them with balance, but you need to use them to push you forward down the trail. Pretend the pole is like a glass of water you're holding. You reach out and hold it in front of you, then place it in the snow and push yourself forward. You ski like you walk, with your feet and hands opposite one another. As your right foot is going forward, your left hand is going forward." Hank waited for them to try.

Then Lucy and Ray tried with the poles. This was a little more complicated, and Lucy soon fell.

"That's good," Hank laughed. "Now I can teach you how to get up."

Lucy was glad there was a trick to it, because otherwise she might be lying there until spring. The more she struggled, the deeper she got in the snow.

"First get your skis parallel. Then take your poles off from the straps and put them together. Hold them in about the middle of the pole and push while you raise yourself to your feet. When you're wearing your pack, take it off before you try to get up." It worked, and soon Lucy and Ray were doing pretty well.

"There are some other skills you'll need for going up and down hills, but I'll teach you those when we get to them. We'll go in the following order: I'll go first to make a trail, then Lucy and Ray, and Bobbie will bring up the rear. Try to stay in the tracks I set. That way, we should have it easy coming back out, unless it snows some more."

Hank gave them each two large water bottles to sling in insulated pouches on the hips of a belt. He encouraged them to drink often and to fill them with snow as the bottles emptied. In spite of the twenty-degree temperatures, they'd be perspiring and would need to stay hydrated to avoid fatigue.

"I don't like the idea of you being first. What if we run into the kidnapper? You're not even armed," Lucy argued.

"Well, we know we're pretty safe for a while. We can talk about switching as you get the hang of skiing some more."

Before they left, Ray went to his truck. Lucy followed. He opened a box in the back. Lucy's eyebrows rose an inch, and her eyes grew wide. In the box was an arsenal of weapons and ammunition. He took out a collapsible rifle similar to the one the Olympians use when they ski and then stop and shoot at targets, but this one looked more powerful. He also took a Smith and Wesson handgun with a holster and gave another one to Lucy with an extra clip of bullets.

Lucy said nothing and Ray just smiled at her expression. She felt the deep respect and affection he held for her.

They all took off on their skis and walked across 55 and into the woods. They started on the snowmobile trail. The snowmobiles had packed down the snow, and the skiing was easy, but still Lucy found it challenging to ski with no snow to keep her feet in line. Her skis crossed over one another and she fell twice in the first mile. She didn't feel too embarrassed or annoyed, though, because Ray fell three times, and even Bobbie fell once. Bobbie was a good skier but she wasn't used to carrying as much weight as she had on her back.

When they made it to their first hill in the woods, Hank taught them how to snowplow. He pointed the tips of his skis in and the back ends out. He proceeded slowly down the hill, his skis splayed out, leaving a track like the big plows that clear the highways of deep snow.

As he skied, Hank felt a strange relief. He was needed. He was valuable. The hardness and anger that had marked his daily life since Scott's death eased and the tension left his body.

Bobbie went next to give them another model. "On the smaller hills, if you feel comfortable, just bend your knees and lean slightly forward at the waist and separate your skis a little more but keep them parallel. You can even double pole if you want more speed, but don't be afraid to take off your skis and walk down if it looks too steep."

Bobbie went down the hill much faster, and by the time she stopped she was halfway up the hill on the other side. Both Ray and Lucy chose the more cautious snowplow, and each fell once going down. Once they reached the bottom, Hank taught them how to herringbone up the other side. This time he pointed the tips of his skis out and the backs in, and he stepped up the hill, slapping his skis as he landed. He placed the poles behind the skis for an extra push. It looked easy enough when Hank did it, but Lucy and Ray had to struggle to make it up the hill, and Lucy was breathing hard by the time she reached the top.

Soon they reached the trail that Ray and Lucy had found the day before. Hank went forward and began making a trail in front of them in the unbroken snow. The going was slower than before, but Lucy and Ray had a path to follow which made skiing easier. Little by little, they began to improve their form. In the powder snow, they began to use the parallel technique down the hills. Soon they were past the point they had reached on snowshoes.

Lucy was so intent on watching the tips of her skis that Bobbie had to remind her to take some time to look around the woods and listen to the quiet. They were far away from any roads now, and everything was white. Lucy had never seen the woods so beautiful. She could see so much farther because the leaves and underbrush were gone in the winter.

They were at the top of a ravine and a herd of deer had gathered at the bottom, three or four hundred yards away. Something seemed to have spooked them, and soon they ran out of sight. At that moment, Lucy remembered that they were after a kidnapper and possible murderer who probably knew these woods a lot better than they did. She spent less time looking at her skis after that. She did not have to remind herself again. She became more alert and focused her attention on any possible clues.

By lunchtime, they had reached a point in the woods that Lucy and even Ray had never seen before. Lunch was simple: trail mix, crackers, cheese, and salami, washed down with water.

They weren't sure where they were. Lucy could tell that everyone was getting tired. Hank was the oldest of the group and was carrying the most weight, but the sled may have made it easier. He had the hardest job, making the track in the front of the group. She knew her own body, and it was screaming at her. Her inner thighs were burning. She looked at Ray and Bobbie and saw fatigue in their faces.

"You need to teach Ray and me how to make a track," she said to Hank. "You have the heaviest load, and it's not fair that you have to bust the trail, too. Besides, we could be skiing right into the sights of a rifle for all we know." Lucy was hoping that was not the case. Though she spoke with confident authority, a shiver went up her spine.

Hank didn't argue. "I don't mind keeping it up, but I'll do what you think is best."

"I think we need to start looking for a place to make camp soon," Ray added. "It'll be dark shortly after four and it's one-thirty now. We'll need light to put up the tent and we need to stay rested in case we catch up to this guy. If there is shooting, we need to be alert, not exhausted."

Lucy shivered once again. It was not from the cold.

They rested awhile after lunch and when they started again, Lucy wished they hadn't. The rest had given her time to get stiff and it was an effort just to move again. The groans of the rest of the group told her they felt the same. Ray took the lead, and they moved more slowly while he got the hang of making the trail. By three o'clock, the sun was getting low in the sky. Every muscle in Lucy's body hurt and she could tell that her long underwear was soaked. She had only cotton long underwear and it held the moisture. Spending the entire day in twenty-degree weather was beginning to take its toll. She felt chilled all the way to her bones.

All day they had been following the kidnapper's tracks that had been covered by several inches of snow. The only way they could discern the tracks was by a tiny dip in the snow out in front of them. Looking over Ray's shoulder, Lucy could see a spot where the tiny dip veered off. She called to Ray who was so busy making their own track that he hadn't noticed what she saw.

Ray calmly pulled his handgun and took off his skis. He went underneath the bushes and disappeared. Lucy pulled her weapon as well. It only took a minute or two, but to Lucy it seemed like ages. Ray returned to the group with a smile.

"We won't have to put up that tent, and I'm pretty sure we're on the right track. Come see this," he said with excitement.

As they took off their skis and scurried under the bushes, they saw a small field. In the middle of it was a mound of snow, and on the opposite side, they saw an entrance to a snow fort similar to an igloo.

They crawled inside the fort. The ground in the fort first went down and then up; this kept more of the cold out of the enclosure. They could see the remains of a fire that was vented through the roof. There was a small table with a plate and silverware, as well as diapers and some bottles. They each smiled at one another. It was a hard day's work, but right now it seemed worth it.

They soon collected wood for a fire. Hank pulled a pot out of his backpack and boiled some snow. When the water began to boil, he opened a bag of freeze-dried chicken and noodle casserole and added it to the water. Everything was in one bag. Within a half hour, it was ready. He reached once more into what seemed like a bottomless bag and produced four tin cups, each about twice the size of a coffee mug and with a long metal handle. Each was filled and handed around for a full portion.

Lucy could have spent hours cooking but the result wouldn't have tasted any better than at that moment. Since she usually didn't sleep well, Lucy was often tired, but she wondered whether she had ever felt this exhausted before. She felt bruised and battered, but she knew she had to go on.

Silently, they all helped clean up, and then they sat around the fire. It had the look of a séance as each of them stared silently into the fire, but their eyes were out of focus, and no one moved. Ray finally broke the spell and pulled Lucy aside.

"I think you and I should take turns keeping watch outside. We don't know if he will return. How about if you take the first watch? It's about eight o'clock now. I'll bring you some coffee when it's ready, then I'll start about ten. We can switch every three or four hours till morning."

Thank God for Ray, Lucy thought. It hadn't even occurred to her to post a watch.

"That sounds good. Come and get me about two, and I'll take the rest of the night. I haven't slept for more than four hours in years. At least my staying awake could serve a purpose for a change." Lucy sounded sarcastic, but her smile was gentle and welcoming.

Hank and Bobbie had volunteered to take a turn at guard duty, but Lucy would have none of it. It was a clear night, and Lucy had never seen so many stars. At eight thirty, Ray came out with coffee and they both watched the Northern Lights put on a show for more than an hour. They called to Hank and Bobbie, and the four of them watched until around nine thirty when Hank and Bobbie were finally persuaded to turn in.

Lucy stayed out until ten, but the night was getting cold with plenty of snow, no wind, and clear skies. It would soon be below zero outside the snow cave. Lucy was shivering as she stripped down to her long underwear and crawled into the sleeping bag. She could tell by their slow rhythmic breathing that Hank and Bobbie were already asleep. She was prepared to keep her regular vigil, staring at new surroundings, and uncomfortable sleeping with other people in the room, but eight hours of skiing caught her and pulled her into a deep sleep.

Just before Ray was supposed to wake her for her watch, she saw a baby's face smiling at her in a dream, and then she felt a cold hand by her face. She woke with a start. Ray put a finger to her mouth and gently shushed her.

"I wish I could let you sleep, but I'm shivering and falling asleep at the same time, and it's bitter cold out there. It's two thirty and below zero. Maybe we can figure our guy is somewhere warm and sleeping now."

"No, I've already set a post-treatment sleep record. I'll keep watch." Lucy's long underwear, which was damp when she got into the sleeping bag, was still wet. When she got out of the bag and hit the air, she began to shiver. As she grabbed her jeans and pulled them on, her hands were now shaking so badly she couldn't button them.

She felt a hand slide over hers. Ray said to her, "Right now, hypothermia is a bigger threat to you than anyone or anything that might be out there. You need to take this underwear off and hang it by the fire so it's dry by the time you put it on in the morning. Then you need to crawl into the bag with me so I can warm you up." Ray pulled his underwear top off so he was bare-chested. He was firm, and she welcomed his strong arms surrounding and holding her.

Lucy had men use a number of lines to get her to bed, but this was a first. "Why are you taking yours off?" It had been a very long time since she had been with a man. She was surprised at the strong stirrings she was feeling.

"Only so my body heat can warm you."

Lucy just smiled an "I'm not buying this" smile.

"Do it. We'll be lying back to front. This is not the time or the place for anything more than that." The thought of something more happening was playing in her mind. She was hopeful that there might be an opportunity in the future.

For the first time, Lucy heard the concern and urgency in his voice. She took off her top leaving only a bra, and then the bottoms leaving her panties. She crawled into Ray's sleeping bag. Just as Ray said, they lay back to front. It was too cold to think much, and Lucy did not want to think. It would make the situation even more awkward. It was not long before she stopped shivering and fell asleep. Ray soon followed.

Hank smiled. He had been resisting the urgings of his bladder for the last half hour. He'd heard the conversation and was ready to add his two cents' worth if Lucy didn't listen. He was glad he didn't need to, and he smiled when he heard the change of breathing indicating they were asleep.

There were newer methods of dealing with early-stage hypothermia, thought Hank with a quiet laugh. Usually you would brew the person some hot tea or soup and have them do jumping jacks to warm up. The interpersonal value of Ray's methods were superior, he decided.

He liked both Ray and Lucy and thought they would make a great couple. He thought of them together for a time until the warmth of his sleeping bag won out, and he fell back asleep.

One other person was left awake. He was standing in the trees just past the clearing. He wore a headlamp now turned off. He waited for another guard to appear, and when none did, he made his move silently and quickly.

chapter 9

IT WAS LIGHT WHEN Hank's bladder could be ignored no longer. The fire had gone out and it was cold inside the cave, but it was sure to be colder outside. He slipped into his pants and shirt and headed outside. The sun was rising over the trees, but it had had little effect on the air temperature. When he stepped out of the cave, suddenly the cold didn't matter to Hank anymore. Little did. Even his bladder no longer held his attention. He wondered if his legs could move.

Blood, lots of blood, covering the snow just outside the snow cave—that was all he could see.

He thought with panic of the people inside. He ran back to Bobbie's bag first. She was lying still and silent—sleeping, he hoped. He shook her gently to make sure. Her eyes opened and she smiled until she saw the fear in his eyes.

"What's the matter?" In a moment she sat up straight, wide awake and alert.

"Stay there for a minute," was all he said. He moved quickly over to Ray and Lucy, still together in the sleeping bag. As he approached them, they both opened their eyes.

"You need to check the outside of the entrance," he said. "Something happened out there, and I don't want to screw up any evidence."

"What's happened?" Lucy asked quickly. Inwardly, she was already kicking herself for not being out there. I would have to pick this night to get my first good night's sleep in four years, she thought with annoyance.

"I just saw what looks like lots of blood in the snow, and I came right back to check on you guys." Hank was rocking back and forth holding his stomach. Lucy was sure it was tied in knots. He looked very pale.

Ray was quickly out of his bag and into his clothes. As if it had not yet occurred to her, Lucy suddenly realized how little she had on. She hesitated getting out of the bag in front of Hank. After a moment, Hank realized her embarrassment and turned around.

Ray had hurried to be the first dressed and stepped out of the snow cave. He stopped abruptly outside the door. Hank was right; there was lots of blood. Ray's blood ran cold at what he saw next—a baby's head stuck to a stake and planted in the snow. He turned away quickly. Then his brain registered that something was wrong. He looked again.

Lucy had followed close behind him and then stood, frozen in her tracks. Ray felt her shaking. She was fighting not to vomit and repeating to herself over and over: "Control your breathing, control your breathing." She couldn't look again.

The baby's face was covered in blood. More blood had dripped on and then frozen to the stake. Ray forced himself to look again, and to look carefully. Then he breathed a sigh of relief. The neck was smooth, with a lip at the bottom of it.

"It's a doll's head," he told Lucy, with another deep sigh.

Lucy opened one eye and looked again. Then she opened both eyes to be sure. A myriad of emotions rushed through her: dread, fear, and relief. Surprisingly, she was not angry yet.

Ray retreated into the snow cave and returned with his rifle. He walked to the point where they had left the trail and looked at the tracks, then walked the perimeter of the field surrounding the cave. He found no other tracks.

"Is it okay to come out?" Hank asked from the doorway.

"Do you still have the bag that dinner came in last night?" Lucy asked, and now it was not difficult to keep her voice calm.

"Yes. It's in a side compartment of my backpack."

"Great. Bring it out, but let me warn you, you're going to be horrified by what you see. It isn't as bad as it seems though."

Hank got the bag and walked out. The blood he had seen before, but not the gruesome stake. Like Ray and Lucy, he looked once, and then looked hurriedly away.

"It's a doll's head," Ray and Lucy said in unison.

Still horrified, Hank looked again. "What's all the blood from?"

"I don't know." Ray said, shaking his head. "What I find even more disturbing is how it all got here. There are no new tracks in the snow other than ours."

Lucy's face turned white. Her mother's words came back to her and softly left her mouth. "You're dealing with powers you don't understand."

Ray took the bag from Hank, stretched over the frozen pool of blood, wrapped the bag around the head and stake, and pulled them from the ground.

Bobbie appeared outside the snow cave for the first time. Her face blanched and she looked very afraid.

"We have to go back," Lucy said.

"That's just what he wants us to do. That's what this whole thing is about," said Hank earnestly. "If he wanted us dead, he could have killed us all in our sleep."

"We don't know what we're dealing with," said Lucy as earnestly, "and we've gone from the hunters to the hunted."

Ray went over and peered more closely at the footprints. "Hank, let me see the bottoms of your boots."

Hank looked confused, but obliged.

Ray looked down at the shoes, then said: "I agree. We need to go back."

"What does that have to do with the bottoms of my shoes?" Hank asked.

"Because he's using our tracks to cover up his own. I bet he used our ski tracks, too."

Hank and Ray looked back toward Lucy but she was looking steadily at Bobbie. Bobbie was still staring at the pool of blood. Hank was thankful that she had missed the doll's head on the stick. Lucy told Bobbie about the bloody warning but avoided details. The description was enough. Bobbie turned very pale.

"We're lucky to be alive, and I don't think we should push it," Lucy insisted, nodding soberly toward Bobbie. "Even if it was a doll's head, he may be saying he'll kill the baby or us if we get any closer."

"I still don't believe he wants to harm that baby," Hank said stoutly. "Do you think he's wandering around in below-zero weather with that baby in a backpack?"

"I don't know," Lucy said.

Then Bobbie spoke. "We have no guarantee that the baby will be safe if we stop looking, either," she said, and her voice was steady. "He may have used the doll's head because the baby's already dead and buried. He can't scare us away like this. Not now that we know we're on his trail. Let's find this guy."

They all turned to Bobbie, marveling over what she had said. Hank especially felt surprised and proud. He knew how afraid she was, and yet she voted to continue. He remembered reading once that the person with the greatest amount of courage is the one who has the greatest amount of fear to overcome. His children continued to amaze and impress him. He thought, as he always did, of his dead son and a strong wave of grief passed quickly over him as Scott's face crossed his mind.

"Well," he said, shaking off sadness and supporting Bobbie, "let's do first things first. We need some coffee and some breakfast; though probably none of us is hungry, we'll need the energy. Then we have to break camp and head back because that's the direction he's going anyway. Let's see what we find. Maybe we'll end up back at Lisa's house," Hank suggested.

Lucy smiled. First things first—a simple AA philosophy, but it usually worked.

"Sounds good," she said.

Hank started a fire and boiled hot water and made coffee. They each drank some of the coffee. Then Hank pulled out several packets of oatmeal. They used their Sierra cups to eat their fill, and then they put everything back into their backpacks and started back the way they had come the day before.

After two days of skiing, Lucy and Ray's skills were much improved. They still fell occasionally on some of the steep hills, but the snow was soft and broke their falls. Hank and Bobbie never fell, and that helped save energy for them because, even with all the techniques Hank was able to teach them, getting back up in the deep snow was hard work.

The skiing was much easier with the trail already established, but the effort of vigilance was greater. Each of them was now aware that the kidnapper knew they were out there and that they were after him. Their eyes constantly scanned the woods, but, unlike the day before, they weren't able to appreciate the beauty. They were all watchful and very determined to find the lunatic who had left that ugly gift for them.

After a few miles of skiing, they reached a grove of pine trees. Ray, who was in the lead with his rifle at the ready, noticed an odd spot in the snow. It might have been a mound of snow that had fallen from the pine tree boughs. It also might have been a spot where the kidnapper left the trail and then attempted to cover his tracks. Ray asked the rest of them to stay back while he moved on alone. He disappeared into the pine trees and was gone for what seemed to be a long time. When he reemerged, they all breathed a sigh of relief.

"Yeah, he was trying to cover his tracks," he announced. "On the other side of the pine trees, it looks like he circled back on a different path."

They all looked at Lucy. "Let's vote," she said.

Soon they were skiing under the pine trees. Now they were following him again, or so they hoped.

THEY FOLLOWED THE tracks carefully and in silence. They had skied for several hours when the tracks led them to a cabin. They all stopped and ducked back under the cover of some pines. They were discussing what to do next when a man appeared outside. Lucy assessed him quickly with her eyes—tall, slender, and decidedly older, with a dark, wrinkled face. He was staggering and had a bottle in one hand and a rifle in the other.

"What do you people want?" he demanded loudly.

"We're police officers," Lucy hollered back. "We'd like to ask you a few questions. Is it okay if we come up?"

"If you're looking for that guy who came through here earlier, he continued down that way." He pointed to some fresh tracks that headed off in the same direction they had been traveling.

"We're cold and hungry. Do you mind if we come in and warm up? We'll pay you for your time," Lucy asked.

There was a pause. Then the man shouted, "Come on in."

Lucy and Ray went first, screening Bobbie and Hank. The man's rifle hung from the crook in his arm, and he never moved it.

"Thanks, …?" Ray said, with a lingering question.

"Ezra," he said. "Ezra Marsh."

In the cabin, he set his gun down on a rack by the door. The inside of the cabin was a single large room with a Franklin stove for heat. The floor was plywood. It had a sink with an old-fashioned pump for water and the drain ran straight out of the house. There was no indoor bathroom and Bobbie asked permission to use the outhouse which was about fifty feet from the cabin.

There was only one chair at the kitchen table and a single bed in the corner. A rocking chair stood by one of the few windows, and there were cans of beans, soup, chili, vegetables, and canned fruit lined on shelves in the kitchen. A deer was hanging from its hind legs from the porch rafters. It looked like a fresh kill.

Hank used the kitchen table to spread out trail mix, salami, and crackers. He invited their tall, silent host to join them for lunch but Ezra simply held up his bottle and said he'd be drinking his lunch.

"I'm chilled to the bone," said Lucy. "How about a hit of that?" She pointed to the bottle.

"Sorry," the man said. "This is my last one, and I have to go all the way to town to get another. Why are you looking for that man?"

"It's not so much the man we're looking for," said Ray. "It's a baby we think he might have. There was a nine-month-old baby taken from town the other night during that big snowstorm. We think he's got the baby."

"Huh," said Ezra, then he fell silent and looked out the window.

"How do you get to town when you go there?" Lucy asked.

"I've got a snowmobile and a truck in a garage at the fire lane, where I'm sure that skier was headed. This time of year, I usually take the snowmobile."

He was quiet again, then asked, "What does a man want with a baby?"

"We don't know," said Ray. "How far is that garage from here?"

"About five miles."

"How do you get to the garage?" Lucy asked.

"I walk or snowshoe."

"How far ahead of us do you think the man on the skis is now?"

"I would guess three or four hours."

"Did he stop here?"

"No, I just saw him go by. Seemed he was in quite a hurry."

"How was he dressed?"

"A lot like you guys. He had a light jacket, but he seemed to have his over his backpack. Now that you mention a baby, he might have been keeping it warm that way."

"How was he built?" Ray asked.

"He seemed tall and thin."

"Where does the fire lane come out?" Lucy asked.

"On highway VV, near Berry Lake."

"How many miles is it on the fire lane to VV?" Hank asked.

" 'Bout eight miles."

"If we start now, we might be able to make it to the fire lane by dark. Your radios should work from there. Maybe you could have someone pick us up."

They gathered the leftover food, said goodbye to Ezra, and left.

As they started down
the path away from Ezra's cabin, Ray continued to lead with his
rifle slung across his arm, and Bobbie went next, still carrying a
larger pack. Hank followed her, and Lucy was in the rear.

Early on in their search, Hank had been fairly chatty on
the trail. Ever since they had found the track to Ezra's cabin, he
had been very quiet. Now he was absolutely silent.

Lucy finally asked him why he was so quiet.

"Aren't we worried about the guy ahead of us?" Hank
replied.

"I'm not, and anyway I don't think that's why you're quiet,"
Lucy answered.

"Okay," Hank answered explosively, as if a cork had been
let out of a bottle. His response had been building pressure
inside for a long time. "Why did you ask that guy for a drink?
You know you can't drink alcohol."

"I'm surprised you of all people would ask me that
question," Lucy said, genuinely confused.

Hank actually stopped and turned around. "Me of all people! What am I supposed to do, just let you relapse?"

She looked at him steadily. "Hank, when you walked into that place where he had been drinking all day, what did you smell?"

Hank was the one confused now. "What did I smell? What does that have to do with you not only relapsing but also putting all our lives in jeopardy because you lose focus and make the wrong decision out here? You're worried about what I smelled? I didn't smell anything." After he said this, Hank paused, suddenly aware of Lucy's point.

They say a shark can smell a drop of blood in ten million gallons of water. A recovering alcoholic is at least as adept at smelling alcohol. Often, it is very repulsive to them and makes them sick. If Ezra had had a bottle of whiskey open in his cabin, not only would there be the smell from the open bottle, but also on his breath. Even his body would be secreting it. But Hank had smelled nothing.

"You knew it wasn't alcohol," he said with a quiet laugh. "How dumb am I, not only for not picking up on that, but also for doubting you. I'm sorry. Can you be sure, besides the smell, that it wasn't booze in there?"

"Well, for one thing, I've never known a self-respecting drunk who was unwilling to share."

Hank thought about this, smiled, and nodded.

"Besides, the bottle he was drinking out of had an old label on it, like the one it had when my father used to drink it. I used to drink the same stuff, and by then the label was different. How long did you keep liquor?"

"I remember once when I had the flu, a case of beer lasted me an entire week. But why would he pretend to be a drunk? I could tell him that it's just not all that glamorous."

"He had to make us think he wasn't out all night stalking us and pouring blood next to us while we slept," Lucy answered. "I'll bet that deer on his porch donated the blood you found this morning. He's our kidnapper."

Hank had started skiing again, but this made him stop and turn around.

"That's the guy? What makes you so sure?"

"Well, for one thing, why else would he pretend to be drunk? And he matches the description that Lisa gave. I bet if we searched underneath that cabin of his we'd find cross-country skis and maybe even a doll without a head."

Bobbie no longer pretended not to listen. "Why don't you arrest him then?" she asked anxiously.

"He obviously doesn't have the baby now. I think if we arrested him, he wouldn't tell us where it is. I'd rather have him think we bought his story, and maybe he'll lead us to where the baby is. What do you think, Ray?"

"I think you are one smart cop, Lucy," said Ray. "I also think I should quit busting my ass trying to catch up with some mythical character ahead of us." He slowed to a stop and took a long drink from his water bottle.

Watching him, Lucy suddenly felt warm all over. She had been so busy since her eyes opened this morning, she never even thought of the night before. It had been so long since she had slept next to a man, but she remembered clearly how comfortable and safe Ray's body felt next to hers.

What she liked even more than that was that she trusted him. He had kept his word, even though she wasn't sure she'd have resisted if he hadn't. She felt secure with him. She'd slept like a baby, safe in his arms. He respected her and wasn't afraid to let other people know that he did. How many other men would have pretended to know what Lucy had figured out regarding this case? Ray gave her all the credit. Now she was beginning to understand some of the feelings she had when she was around him. First was confusion. She had never known a man like Ray Waupuse. Second was also confusion, but of a different kind: she had never felt what she felt toward him, not even toward her husband, God rest his soul.

"Hey, Lucy!" called Bobbie, rousing her out of her daydreams. "Come on over and take a break with us."

They each rested awhile on the trail and drank some water. Hank pulled out some trail mix, and they snacked on it. Then they heard a snowmobile in the distance.

They were close now to where Ezra said he kept a snowmobile and they wondered if he had slipped out ahead of them on another trail. They quickly packed their gear and continued down the trail. When they arrived at the fire lane, they looked for the shed where Ezra stored his snowmobile and truck. Both the snowmobile and truck were still there. Ray felt the motors and they were cold.

Lucy pulled out her radio and tried to reach someone, but all she heard was silence. It was getting dark, and now the question was what to do next.

"Should we pitch a tent and stay out here another night, or use our headlamps and go the eight more miles to VV?" Hank asked.

It was nearly six in the evening and already getting dark.

"Eight miles seems like a lot of skiing, especially in the dark," Ray said.

"I agree. I'm pretty tired, but I don't relish the idea of pitching a tent and being a sitting duck for some wacko either," Bobbie added.

"We can keep going and keep trying the radio. As we get closer, we're bound to be able to reach the station or a squad going by on VV," Lucy said.

"We might meet up with someone on a snowmobile on this fire lane also. I know I've been on this stretch myself," said Ray. "There are some bars on VV that they frequent," he added.

"That's another thing that scares me, speaking of being sitting ducks," said Hank. "We've got to be careful of some drunken snowmobiler heading down the lane at a hundred miles an hour."

They turned on their headlamps and started cautiously down the lane. They had skied for about an hour and had gone a few miles when they heard a snowmobile behind them. Lucy immediately thought of Ezra. He could easily hit them and say he hadn't seen them in the dark.

"Let's move off the lane," she yelled to those ahead. They moved, but the snowmobile quickly closed the gap between them. When the rider caught them, he stopped.

"Teller, is that you?" The man on the sled was wearing a helmet with a face shield, but Lucy had no difficulty identifying Lieutenant Moon's voice.

"Yes, sir," she answered.

"We've been looking for you for hours now and trying to contact you on your radio. Do you have it on?"

"No, sir. I was trying to save the battery. Also, it was not working." She wondered if he had his glasses on under his helmet and if he was looking over them right now.

"Speaking of the battery, when was the last time you changed it?" Lieutenant Moon asked firmly.

"It might have been awhile, sir." She felt herself flushing, but it didn't matter. It was too dark for him to see, and no matter what, she had never been happier to see anyone.

The Lieutenant used his radio, and soon there were enough snowmobiles to get them to VV, into squad cars, and back to their cars at Dawn's house. Hank found Bobbie's cell phone and called Molly to let her know they were both all right. Neither he nor Bobbie felt capable of driving the hour home without risking falling asleep at the wheel, and Lucy had asked them to help her with her report in the morning.

Hank promised to fill Molly in as soon as he arrived home. He told his wife he loved her and said goodbye. Ray lived alone and had room at his place for them to stay the night. While Hank and Bobbie took turns using the shower, Ray cooked some food, and it smelled delicious. Their mouths were watering as the three of them sat down to eat. Bobbie and Hank cleaned the dishes while Ray took his turn in the shower. They watched TV for a while afterwards, but none of them was able to make it through the first show.

One by one, as their dreams awoke them, they made their way to bed. It was well past dawn before their feet touched the floor again.

Lucy, meanwhile, had gone home and spent the better part of an hour soaking in the tub, occasionally adding more hot water.

When she got out, there were four people who were anxious to hear what she had found. She left out all that they had discovered after their first night in the woods, but for Lisa, she gave enough information to help her believe there was still hope of finding her brother alive.

For her children, she talked about skiing and the spot where they had spent the night in the ice house. She told them all the things she had learned about winter camping and surviving in the woods. She kept to herself what she had discovered about her feelings toward Ray. There was no reason even to mention their sharing of his sleeping bag.

When she finally crawled into her own bed, she wondered what would await her. She had so much to review and so many decisions to make about what to do next, but she knew also that she was exhausted and needed rest. What would win: her tired-to-the-bone body, her head full of thoughts and ideas clamoring for her attention, or her newly awakened feelings waiting to be explored? A wave of sleep washed over all of it, giving her body the rest it needed, and leaving her unconscious mind to sort out everything else. The result was a series of bizarre dreams, most of which she couldn't remember later. They were capped by a nightmare that, unfortunately, she did remember, of a smiling, contented baby stuck on a stake. It was so horrific, it woke her.

Still shaky, she got up, made some coffee, and started her report.

chapter *12*

WHEN SHE GOT HOME,
Bobbie decided to drive in to see Kathy Marks, Scott's old
girlfriend. The two of them had become especially close since
her brother's death. Kathy had kept in touch with Lucy too. In
fact, she had spoken with her a few days earlier and volunteered
to take Lisa to school.

Kathy was now working in the same classroom where Scott
had worked before he died. She felt a special connection to
Scott there. When she heard about it, Kathy was disappointed
she hadn't been able to join them in the search for Lisa's
brother. She and Brad Albert—Scott's best friend and hers—
had begun to date regularly now, but she hadn't told Bobbie yet.
She felt a bit awkward about it, as if Bobbie would think she
had betrayed Scott by recovering from his death and falling in
love with someone else.

Bobbie also withheld a great deal, since she wasn't
sure what Lucy would want her to reveal about an ongoing
investigation. Kathy talked about her experiences with the

children, and Bobbie was quite interested in that, since she had been an education major herself and had thought she'd go back to it when she returned to school. She was also toying with the idea of a criminal justice career after her experience over the last couple of days.

She told Kathy she had never been so frightened in all her life, but she felt that she had never been involved in anything more meaningful or exciting.

She thought about this very long and hard on her way over to Lucy's house. It really was an extraordinary experience, Bobbie thought. And perhaps it was her opportunity to recover from Scott's death. Without knowing all that Kathy had withheld about Brad, Bobbie had still noticed how well Kathy was looking. She wanted to look that well too. She began to think of her boyfriend, Tom, and her mind wandered off.

Bobbie was still driving back when Hank sat down with Lucy and read what she had written in her report. There wasn't much he could add or alter since he agreed with what she had written.

"Of course," he said, "I don't see anything in here about Officer Teller faking hypothermia so she could crawl in the sack with Officer Waupuse." Hank laughed and Lucy turned red. "You know, I was just going to give you the same advice if you hadn't agreed with Ray. As a matter of fact, if you hadn't stopped shaking I was prepared to wake Bobbie and have her strip to her bra and panties and get in front of you in the bag.

Hypothermia is nothing to take lightly. If you had finished dressing and gone outside, I'm convinced you'd be dead right now. Ray saved your life. I like him a lot, Lucy, and I like the two of you together. Not that it's any of my business, or that you care about my opinion."

Lucy smiled. "I do care what you think, but I have to simplify my life a little before I can think about adding anything more to it," she said. Then, partly to change the subject, she asked, "Had any more dreams about Scott lately?"

During the investigation of Scott's death, both she and Hank had dreamed about Scott many times. They had shared these dreams with each other—helping greatly in the investigation.

"No," said Hank. "I haven't dreamed about Scott. I wake up every morning feeling disappointed that he hasn't visited me again. I can't tell you what it meant to me to have the opportunity to do this with you over the last couple of days. Not only did I get a chance to prove something to myself, but also I was able to get out of myself for a while and away from my own grief and guilt. How about you?"

"No. I guess like you I've focused on finding Michael and haven't focused on Scott as much. But I have the feeling that we're doing what Scott wants us to do."

"The next right thing—that's what both of us have to remember, I guess," Hank said.

Bobbie walked in on the last of the conversation. "I've come to know AA talk when I hear it. What is this about?" she asked.

Lucy gave Hank an "I defer to you" look.

"We were talking about Scott," Hank said.

"Oh," was all Bobbie said, and she looked down.

An awkward silence filled the room—at least, awkward for Hank and Bobbie who were used to the room being filled with words when three people were present.

Bobbie broke the silence. "So should I look at your report?" she asked Lucy.

Lucy handed it to her, and she began to read.

After a few minutes, Bobbie handed the report back to Lucy. "It looks pretty thorough," she said. Then she made a few small suggestions. Lucy thanked her, and Bobbie was pleased at the thanks.

On the ride home, Hank and Bobbie talked openly about what they had shared together. They felt closer as father and daughter than they had since long before Scott's death. Even more wonderful, when they reached home, the whole family was there to greet them.

"What are you doing here?" demanded Hank with a laugh as Ryan appeared in the doorway.

"I'm low on laundry," Ryan replied with a broad grin. "You don't think I would come home just to see you people, do you?"

They all talked for a long time, heartily, and even, at times, all at once. But, underneath, they were all apprehensive because the baby was still missing.

AT THE TREATMENT center, Lucy's first stop was in Dr. Wolf's office. He was there, riding an exercise bike in the corner. He had run cross-country in high school and was pretty good at it. Then, with medical school and his drug involvement, he had gotten very out of shape. Now, partly to relieve the stress of working with addicts all day, he had started running again. As he began to regain his former condition, he had gotten into cross-training. He not only ran, but also started bike riding, rollerblading, canoeing, and swimming. He had won a few of the 5K races the tribe sponsored during the powwow. He had also won the reservation's first triathlon the previous summer. He had even gotten a group together to put on an "experience the rez" event for the following summer. Like one held in Duluth, Minnesota, it would involve not only the swimming, biking, and running of a triathlon, but also canoeing, kayaking, rollerblading, and mountain biking.

"How's my favorite patient?" he asked, not slowing down his pedaling in the least, keeping up a cadence of ninety repetitions per minute.

"Oh, you say that to all the girls, Dr. Meany," Lucy said, in a tone of mock dejection. "How is our new favorite patient doing?"

"I think you'll be pleasantly surprised. She's been going to group, and they've been calling her on her lack of responsibility, and getting her to deal with her feelings honestly. She's sure not out of the woods yet, and you know the recovery rate of heroin addicts, but I'd say she has a fighting chance. Any news on her son?"

"Nothing concrete." Lucy didn't want to burden Dr. Wolf with details that he would then have to keep from everyone else. "I do believe that the baby is still alive. By the way, I've got a great new aerobic exercise for you to try. We've been searching the woods on cross-country skis, and I now have to use my arms to lift my legs to operate the clutch and brake on my truck; that's how sore my legs are."

"I've tried the machines a few times, but never the real thing. I understand it's the best aerobic exercise you can get. I'm surprised you're that sore. Aren't you in pretty good shape? You've been telling me you run twenty miles a week."

"I thought I was. I guess it used different muscles, but I sure feel it."

"Well, do you think you're good enough to give me a lesson?"

"I don't know if I am, but I'm sure my friend Hank is. Maybe we could arrange an outing for the alumni group. I know a great trail we could try near here, or we could head up to Hank's. There are a bunch of them up his way, he tells me."

"That sounds like a plan."

"I might even get my kids to try it. We could make it a family outing. I have to get some time off though. Do you know if Dawn is free now?"

Dr. Wolf looked at his watch. "She should be just getting out of group. You know where they meet. I have five more minutes left on this. Stop by on your way out."

Lucy walked down the familiar hall and thought about how her life had changed over the last four years. She had spent the first two getting sober and taking care of her children. After that, she had started working for the tribal police. She had spent one year as a dispatcher and the last as a patrol officer.

At her AA meetings, the question sometimes came up: if scientists invented a pill that allowed you to use socially, would you go back to drinking and using? Lucy was convinced that, even if she was guaranteed that it would work, she wouldn't try it. She liked what she had too much. And anyway, as a Native, she didn't know what social drinking even was.

She smiled to herself. Every drinker she had ever known drank to get drunk. And she didn't know anyone from any culture who took drugs socially—and certainly not heroin.

As she approached the group room, she could see Dawn walking with several other patients with whom she seemed to have made friends. Even from a distance, Lucy could see the change in Dawn. She was arm in arm with another woman, and they were laughing together. She looked like a completely different person. What a change a smile can make, Lucy thought.

When Dawn saw Lucy, the smile left her face.

"Do you have news about my children?" she asked, rushing toward Lucy.

"Well, I can tell you that Lisa's doing okay at home with my family. I talked with her teacher just before I came here, and she's doing well at school too. I wish I had good news about Michael, but I don't have any bad news either. I can't give you details, but I'm more optimistic about Michael than I was the last time I was here."

Then Lucy braced herself for a barrage of criticism and questions that never came.

Dawn looked relieved. "I appreciate what you're doing for all of us," was all she said.

"You seem much better than you were the last time I was here. How has treatment been going?"

"I've got a lot to deal with. As I get the drugs out of my system, I realize more and more why I took them. I have issues with my own growing up that I never addressed, and I used drugs to dull the pain. I looked for a relationship that would keep me safe, and instead I found someone who used me like my father did."

She took a deep breath, then continued. "The counselors are suggesting a halfway house after this so I can continue to deal with all this. They say if I don't take that extra time to heal, the pain of it will lead me right back to using. But how can I abandon my children any longer? I feel like I have so much to make up to them. I don't understand why I never saw this clearly until now."

"Lisa is fine staying with us," said Lucy, "and as of now we don't know where Michael is. So you go ahead and concentrate on living one day at a time and keep healing. Each day without drugs, your mind will get clearer, and you'll see the path you need to take."

Dawn smiled. "You sound like Dr. Meany."

"You know, I'm the one who gave him that name," said Lucy with a laugh. "And now, telling me that I sound like him is really the nicest thing you could have said."

Lucy gave her a goodbye hug and walked back down the hall.

Lucy stuck her head in his office. Dr. Wolf was toweling himself off.

"You're doing a wonderful job, and she says I sound just like you," Lucy said.

The doctor responded with a "thumbs up" and a grin.

A DAY OR SO LATER, Bobbie sat on a snowmobile in a clump of pine trees right near the shed where Ezra kept his snowmobile. Neither Lucy nor Lieutenant Moon was very thrilled with the idea of a civilian doing surveillance, but they didn't have enough officers to watch the shed 24-7 so when Hank and Bobbie offered to help, they had reluctantly agreed. Hank told Lucy that she'd be doing him a favor not only because he wanted to continue to help, but as he put it, he needed help with his daughter as well.

"The good news is she's now anxious to return to school. The bad news is that since our adventure she's considering switching her major to law enforcement. I figure if you can put her on a boring stakeout, maybe she'll find out that a lot of police work isn't so glamorous. Besides, it's not like you want us to confront Ezra, just to find out where he's going."

Hank and Bobbie were both given strict orders to give Ezra plenty of room and make sure they weren't discovered. Lucy gave them fully charged radios that were powerful enough to reach the dispatcher. They each took four-hour daytime shifts.

Bobbie had been sitting behind the trees for about an hour, and though she was dressed for the worst, the bitter cold of the day was already beginning to seep through her snowmobile suit and the layers she had under it. Her mind wandered to her boyfriend, Tom. She had gotten used to seeing him every day, and she missed him since she wasn't at school. They talked every day on the phone, but it wasn't the same. She smiled as she thought of him telling her he was going to parties every night. First, she knew he was teasing, and she had enough spies to let her know he hung around mostly with his friends and was studying hard. Second, she trusted him completely. Tom was not a partier.

She didn't even see Ezra enter his shed and was startled to hear his snowmobile fire up. After warming it up for a while, he drove out. He sped quickly by the trees where she was hiding and seemed to pay little attention to anything around him. She could tell by his speed as he passed that she'd have no trouble giving him plenty of room, because there was no way she was going to be going that fast. She just hoped that she'd have the nerve to go fast enough to be able to tell where he might be going. It had snowed an inch or two the night before, and he was the first to use the logging road, so she didn't have to stay that close.

She radioed that Ezra was on the move and that she was following cautiously behind him. Bobbie was careful to use the word "cautiously" because she knew Ray, Lucy, and her dad would all be listening. Lucy, waiting in her squad car, turned on her dome lights and headed up VV toward Berry Lake, hoping to reach the spot where Ezra would get on the highway. As she got close to the spot where he would exit the woods, she turned off her lights and slowed down.

Soon she saw a flash cross the highway and quickly disappear in the woods on the other side. A few minutes later, Bobbie appeared in the same spot and stopped on the highway. Lucy pulled up in front of her.

"Where did he go?" Bobbie asked.

"He headed straight across the highway. Do you want me to take it from here?"

"No, you're not dressed for it," Bobbie answered. "I'll follow him."

Before Lucy could argue with her, Bobbie was around her car and across the highway.

The minutes passed until she had been following Ezra's tracks for nearly an hour. She occasionally stopped her sled and turned off her engine to listen for other sleds in the area. She could hear one or more, but usually at a distance from her. The sun was dropping low in the sky, and Bobbie wondered if she should turn on her headlight or not. She picked up speed to try to gain on Ezra. Just past a clump of pines, another sledder cut in front of her, and she turned sharply to avoid him. In the next instant, she was heading for a large tree. She turned sharply again and the sled turned, but it was sliding sideways toward the tree now.

Bobbie felt things moving in slow motion even though the sled was moving at a dangerously fast speed. She leaned on it, trying to avoid hitting the tree, and turned the sled on its side. She hit the tree with her runners, and the impact knocked her radio into the snow and the breath out of her lungs.

Bobbie lay in the snow motionless, as darkness fell around her. Even if she could yell, no one would hear her. Bobbie lost consciousness. The snowmobiler who had cut her off continued down the trail, either oblivious of what had happened or intentionally leaving her to freeze in the cold night air.

THE RADIO HAD BEEN silent too long. Hank had started his shift shortly after he had heard that Ezra had crossed VV. He drove his SUV to a parking lot near where Bobbie had crossed VV and pulled his sled off the trailer. Bobbie had radioed a couple of times since crossing VV when she'd stopped her sled to listen, but he had heard nothing for an hour. Night was beginning to settle, and his headlight lit the trail in front of him, but the woods on either side of him were dark.

Lucy and Ray, also concerned, were out on the trail, searching less now for Ezra than for Bobbie. The three of them radioed back and forth, each with nothing to report and hoping their fears would not become reality.

Bobbie came to slowly. At first, she was only distantly aware of the cold on her face. Her foot was wedged under an exposed root and the sled was on top of her leg. Surprisingly, she felt no pain. She could see the radio half-buried in the snow and reached for it, but it was inches beyond her fingertips.

Straining her willpower, she stretched with all her might, but she could not reach it. She could hear Ray, Lucy, and Hank talking amongst themselves, but she couldn't talk to them.

They were coming up the path she had followed, Bobbie heard with relief. When they got near where she was, she began to yell, but the noise from their sleds drowned out her call for help, and between the darkness and the branches of the tree, she was completely blocked from their view. The tears ran down her face as she watched them turn the way that the other snowmobile had gone, far away from where she was. She felt the cold seeping into her, and she fought the urge to fall asleep. She knew she had to stay awake to survive.

After what seemed like eternity to her, alone in the dark and giving up hope, a snowmobile pulled up next to her. A tall, thin man got off the sled and walked toward her.

"I know you guys want to find that baby, but do you really think you're going to find it under that tree in the dark?"

Bobbie panicked when she heard Ezra's voice and lunged as hard as she could for the radio. She touched it with her fingertips just as Hank's voice rang from the speaker. She could hear the fear in her father's voice.

"Bobbie, if you can hear this, please respond."

Ezra picked up the radio. He stared at it for a long time. Bobbie was sure he was contemplating throwing it into the woods. She started to pray silently. Finally, he turned to her.

"How do you work this thing?"

Bobbie started crying. "Push the red button to talk," she said through her tears. "Then let it up to listen."

Ezra did as he was told. "This is Ezra. I've got your daughter. She seems scared and might have a broken leg, but otherwise she's okay."

There was silence on the phone. Ezra turned to Bobbie. "I don't think it worked." He set the radio on his sled.

"Press the button again. Tell them you found me under a tree and that my snowmobile had fallen on top of me."

This time Ezra ignored her. Bobbie heard him say, "I think we need to check you out first. This might hurt." Again without waiting for an answer, he dislodged Bobbie's leg. Probably because it was numb, the pain was bearable.

"You're bleeding," Ezra noted. "The pressure of the sled and the cold kept you from bleeding to death. I need to fix this cut right away." He went right to his sled and pulled out a first aid kit. He took his head lamp and a needle and thread and, before Bobbie's astonished eyes and ignoring her faint protests, began to sew the skin of her ankle. He worked patiently but quickly. When he finished, he took gauze and wrapped the leg tightly.

"Now pull yourself out from there, and I'll straighten out your sled and see if I can't get it started."

Bobbie pulled herself out of what might have been her grave, but remained on the ground, afraid to test the leg. Then Ezra quickly picked up the sled with what appeared to Bobbie to be incredible strength. He started it and pulled it back out to the path. "Can you stand on that leg?"

Bobbie said she could, but she sat in the snow waiting while Ezra tried the radio once more. "This is Ezra again. I found your daughter under a tree. She had an accident. Her leg was stuck under her sled."

This time, the response was immediate and Hank's voice was full of eagerness, gratitude, and nerves: "Where are you, and how can we find you?"

"I'll fire my rifle in the air. Let me know if you hear it."

It was then that Bobbie noticed Ezra had his rifle strapped over his shoulder again. He removed it with one hand. Bobbie watched as he raised the barrel to her face. She closed her eyes and flinched as she heard the shot. When she opened her eyes, he was holding the rifle straight up in the air. "Did you hear that?"

"Yes." It was Lucy who answered. "Fire it again in about a minute."

Bobbie stood up slowly, keeping the weight on her good leg, and then slowly placing weight on the other leg. It felt sore, particularly by the ankle, but it supported her body. She walked to her sled, and Ezra vacated it as she approached. He went to his rifle and fired it in the air again.

"We saw the discharge that time," Lucy said over the radio. "We'll be there in a minute."

"Why don't you let go of this hunt before someone gets hurt? Maybe the baby's in a better place." After saying that,

Ezra threw the radio to Bobbie. "Get inside right away," he told her.

"Thanks," she said.

Then Ezra got on his sled and left.

HANK, LUCY, AND RAY arrived moments after Ezra left. Hank jumped off his snowmobile almost before it stopped and grabbed Bobbie in a rough hug.

"Am I glad to see you," she said, her voice cracking.

"And I you. What happened?"

"Let's get her to my place by the fire, and then we can ask her questions," Ray said with concern in his voice.

All of a sudden, and for the first time since Ezra had arrived, Bobbie realized how cold she was. Hank helped her to climb on her sled. She started to shiver as the speed of her sled created a wind on her body, but the heat from the motor soon began to warm her. Ray went ahead to start his car. As soon as Bobbie arrived in the parking lot, Ray took her into the car, and she sat there with the heater running high while the rest of them loaded up the snowmobiles.

"Ezra said something about a broken leg?" Lucy said with a question in her voice.

"I wedged my foot in an exposed root, and the sled fell on top of my leg. My ankle is sore, but I know nothing is broken. He talked to you after he had gotten me loose, but before I stood up. I had a cut on my leg and he stitched it up. He said if it wasn't for the cold and the pressure my leg was under, I probably would have bled to death."

They made a quick stop at the tribal clinic just to make sure the leg wasn't broken, and to have the doctor look at the stitches.

"I couldn't have done better myself," he said. "Who did this?"

"Ezra Marsh," Lucy answered.

"That explains it. He was a medic in Vietnam. He has a number of awards."

Lucy thought back to his cabin. Any awards were definitely not displayed. She asked the doctor what else he knew about Ezra.

"I've never even met him," he said. "I just heard that he was an Army hero and a medic."

The x-rays were negative.

Once at Ray's, Bobbie wrapped up in a blanket.

"How did you tip?" Hank asked, finally.

"I reached a point where two trails merged. I didn't have my lights on even though it was getting dark because I didn't want Ezra to know where I was. Another sled came from the other direction, and I swerved to avoid him. Then I was heading toward a tree and had to swerve again to avoid it. That's when the sled and I tipped."

"The guy you avoided didn't stop?" Lucy asked.

"I'm not even sure he knew I was there. I came from behind some pine trees. I was slightly behind him, and I didn't have my light on."

"How could anyone not know?" Hank asked in disgust.

"I told you there are several bars on VV. These guys go from one to the next and have several drinks at each one. He could have hit his mother head-on and not known it," Ray said.

"But it could have been Ezra, too," Lucy said. "Do you know for sure it wasn't him?"

"No. As I said, it was getting dark. All I saw was a shadow. But why would he wait over an hour to come back?"

"Maybe his conscience began to get to him, or maybe he just waited around to see if we'd find you first. It could have been another one of his little messages, like the blood and the doll's head."

Bobbie shivered. This time it wasn't from the cold. "I don't know what to think. I have to feel grateful to him for helping me, but I got the strong feeling he was trying to intimidate me too. I know the man gives me the creeps. I don't trust him at all."

"Well, there's no sense in keeping tabs on him now," said Lucy. "He knows we're watching him."

"I'm sorry I blew it," Bobbie said, sounding dejected.

"You didn't do anything wrong. I'm sure he's been suspicious of us since we went to his cabin. Maybe we need to let him think we've heeded his warning and are staying away. I have some other leads I can follow. He's been in this area for a while. He must come into town for supplies. This is a small area. Someone must recognize him. That way we'll get some more information without pressing Ezra directly."

The others agreed and Ray even repeated after her, "Someone must recognize him."

Both he and Lucy would be surprised at just who that someone would be.

chapter 17

THE NEXT DAY, LUCY
decided to see Karen. Karen knew more people in the area than
anyone and always had her ear to the ground. The best she
hoped for was that Karen knew someone who knew someone
who knew Ezra, but as soon as she mentioned Ezra and where
he lived, Karen was on a roll. Lucy didn't even have to tell her
why she was interested in Ezra.

"Oh, yeah, I know him. There was a time he could drink
you and half the village under the table. He was abusive to his
wife and his daughter. He learned to be mean from his own
parents. I've heard he was beaten as a child and came close
to death on two occasions. Finally, his wife got the nerve to
take the daughter and go to a shelter. Ezra, like all abusive
men, promised to change. Said he'd quit drinking, brought her
presents.

"Finally, against all her domestic violence counselors'
advice, she agreed to give him one more chance. Her counselors
were sick about it because the large majority of abusers never

change. They had all too often seen women go back with their heads filled with promises, only to be abused again or worse. But to their surprise, Ezra straightened out. He gave up drinking and became a devoted husband and father. What made it even more amazing is he did it without help. He never attended AA or group counseling for his abuse.

"I stayed involved with the family for years afterward because I always believed he wouldn't last. I kept encouraging him to get help, but he never did. There wasn't a whole lot I could say about it, because not only was there no evidence of problems, but also I believe they were a loving couple and family.

"When their daughter went off to nursing school, they left the reservation to be close to her. They moved back a couple of years ago, when their daughter got a job in Shawano. They were doing great. I'd see him and his wife out cross-country skiing in the wintertime. They had picked it up while their daughter was in college.

"Then Ezra's wife got breast cancer and died quickly. I went to the funeral. Ezra didn't say a word to anyone. He just stared. After the funeral, he moved to his hunting shack in the woods, and I haven't seen him since. I think all that untreated alcoholism finally got the best of him. He never completely escaped the emotional wounds inflicted by his parents and himself."

"What about the daughter? What happened to her?"

"She met a man in college of whom the parents were quite fond. They settled in Shawano, and she still works at a hospital there."

Without quite knowing why, but with a sense that it was somehow important, Lucy asked, curious, "What unit does she work in?"

Karen hung her head. In a soft, sad voice, she answered, "She works in maternity. She's so good with those babies. She and her husband have been trying for so long to have a child. They've even tried a fertility clinic, but now they've given up. It's so sad. She'd be such a good mom."

Light bulbs were flashing in Lucy's head. "When did you find out they had given up?"

"Just last week. She even said she might give up maternity nursing because it's just too painful for her. She told me her husband was getting promoted and it might require a move. She said she might take the opportunity to train in a new area of nursing. Might even go back to school for her master's degree and take some time off."

"Where does she live in Shawano?" Lucy asked.

"I've never been to her house, but she told me once she lives on Loon Lake. It's north and east of there. You know how nice it is around that lake." Karen frowned. "Why..." she began, then stopped and turned pale. After a moment she finished the question: "Why are you so interested in his daughter?"

"Do you suppose you could introduce me to her?" Lucy asked in her turn, standing up quickly.

"Sure. I talked with her this morning about a cocaine baby that was born there. I'm on my way over now, but what's the big deal with her?"

"One more question. Was Michael Lake born in Shawano Hospital, and was Ezra's daughter his nurse?"

Karen's face blanched white. The puzzle she was putting together inside her head was beginning to make a scene she didn't care for.

She took a deep breath, then responded firmly. "Her name is Gabby. She thought Michael was the cutest thing. He stayed in the hospital longer because of low birth weight. She got really attached to him and often asked me about him. She always looked sad or angry when I'd tell her about his family situation. Once she even blurted out, 'It's not fair.' I never thought much about it, because I felt the same way. She seemed concerned when I first told her Michael was missing, but the next time I talked with her about it, she said, 'I'm sure the mother or the boyfriend killed him,' and she didn't seem to want to talk about it any more. I thought at the time it was just too painful for her, but now I see where you're going with this."

"I think Ezra is still trying to make up for what he's done to his wife and daughter, and now she's in a bind," Lucy said. "Let's go see Gabby at the hospital and hint to her that we know what happened. Do you think there's any chance she would hurt the baby to save her father?"

"No. And I'd stake my life on that," Karen said. Then she continued to look thoughtfully at Lucy.

"What?" Lucy asked, because she knew the look.

"Will you have to charge Gabby with aiding and abetting or something like that?"

"That's not up to me."

"But right now, you and I are the only ones who've figured this out, right?"

"We don't even know for sure that we're right. Why?"

"If the baby is in her home, and my gut tells me you're right and he is, and she's charged with a crime, then I'm going to have to remove the baby and take him somewhere else. That would mean removing that child from the best possible environment to someplace less suitable. She's a caring and loving person, and this baby has been through enough. Let's think about him for a while. Can't we at least slow things down? Let me talk with her myself. Let her know I'm on her side and that I think you might be onto what's going on with the baby. You go talk with the mother, tell her the situation, find out what she wants. If she's still in treatment, the baby needs to stay somewhere. Why not where he is?"

Lucy's mind was whirling. "But is it helpful to Gabby to allow her to become even more attached if eventually she's going to have to give him up? Wouldn't it be better to remove him right away?"

"I don't know. My first thought is for the child. Failure to thrive children can sometimes turn around in the right environment. Let's give him a chance at a healthy life," she pleaded.

"All right," Lucy said, slowly. "At least, all right for now. I'll go talk with my sponsor and Dr. Wolf and see what they suggest about talking with Dawn. Make sure you stress to Gabby that if she and her husband do something stupid like take the baby across state lines, it will be out of my hands, and I'll have to report it to the FBI. By the way," she said with a wry smile, "they call it reactive attachment disorder now."

Karen waved her hand in disgust. "I gave up trying to keep up with unimportant changes years ago. I think Gabby will be relieved if there is a way out of this for all concerned. Besides, I'm not powerless in this either. If Gabby provides the best environment for that child, and we're not tied by criminal charges, Michael just may stay there. The judges around here will listen to me."

"You're getting way ahead of me. I think you are still kicking yourself for not acting fast enough, and now you're trying to act too fast. Breathe, Karen, breathe."

"I hate it when my client becomes my counselor. But, you're right. I promise not to get ahead of you in this. I appreciate you giving me some time."

They talked about exactly what Karen would say to Gabby. Once their plans were clear, Karen gave Lucy a hug. "You have been a gift in my life, Lucy Teller."

Lucy smiled with pride. "Funny, I always thought it was the other way around."

Each went her way with a task neither wanted.

chapter 18

LUCY DECIDED TO INCLUDE Ray in on the plan as well since he could advise her in police matters. She called him and asked him to meet her at Maehnowesekiyah. On her way there, she stopped by the house of her sponsor, Sophie, and found her at home.

"Hey, girl," she said in greeting, "I need you to take a ride with me. Are you up for it?"

"I don't know," Sophie snapped, but not too harshly, "I usually don't make a habit of riding with strangers."

"Oh, cut it out. It hasn't been that long."

"Sure, I'll go. Where to?"

"I need to talk with Dr. Wolf out at the treatment center. I'll fill you in on the way."

"Told you you'd relapse if you weren't careful." She stuck out her tongue at Lucy.

"It's not about me. I'm fine."

On the way to the treatment center, Lucy told Sophie everything she could concerning Lisa, Michael, and Dawn. As they pulled up, they spotted Ray waiting for them out front. When they had gathered in Dr. Wolf's office, Lucy explained what she had talked about with Karen.

"I think the baby is in the right place for now, but I don't know what will happen if I tell Dawn I found the baby and then suggest he stay where he is for now."

"What is the purpose of all of us being here?" Ray asked.

"Dr. Wolf is here to help decide what is best for Dawn; besides, it's his office. He'd be here anyway. Sophie is here to help me decide what's best for me and my recovery. You're here to advise me what's best from a police standpoint."

"Well," Sophie said, "I bet Ray and I agree. It sounds like you're taking the law into your own hands, and I say it's dangerous for you personally and professionally. Dawn has come a long way even since you saw her last, but I don't know if she could handle hearing that you want to leave her son with a person who was an accomplice in a kidnapping."

"What if we tell her that we found the baby and put him in foster care for now? It's partly true, and I could be the one to tell her so the treatment staff doesn't have to be a part of a half-truth."

"You still haven't answered my question about taking the law into your own hands. Now you're adding dishonesty to my concerns about you," Sophie said, rolling her eyes and stepping away from Lucy.

"I think at the very least, you need to include Lieutenant Moon in on this," Ray added, moving much closer to Lucy.

"Well," said Lucy, "you are both here to help me decide on priorities. Who should we talk to first, and what should we say? We have to tell Dawn something. We have to tell Lieutenant Moon something. I'd like to tell Lisa about her brother as well, and at this point we're not even sure that Michael is where I think he is." Lucy's head was beginning to hurt. She wished life were simpler.

For a long time the room grew silent. This would be strange in the white culture, but Lucy and the others let the silence settle over them like a warm blanket on a cold night and waited for it to provide the answers. When they spoke again, the room was calmer, and they were working together, speaking with one voice. Between the voices and the silence, a plan emerged, and the values of honesty and respect took charge. They decided to wait awhile longer to tell Dawn until they were sure Lucy was correct. Ray would talk to Lieutenant Moon. They would let Karen talk with Ezra's daughter, and then Lucy would bring Lisa to visit her brother if indeed he was where Lucy thought he was. She could then bring Lisa to visit Dawn, and together they could tell her that her son was safe. Lucy was satisfied with the plan, but looked forward to the time when it would all be finished and she wouldn't have time to worry about it all in advance.

Before they could leave the parking lot, the dispatcher called and told Ray he and Lucy should report immediately to Lieutenant Moon's office. "And he's not happy," she added.

Lucy dropped off Sophie and met Ray outside the Lieutenant's office.

Lucy felt better walking into the Lieutenant's office with Ray, but her good feeling was short-lived when she saw Agent Scruggs of the FBI standing next to the large desk, looking even more smug than usual. Before Lieutenant Moon had a chance to say anything, Agent Scruggs started in.

"While you were busy with your little witch hunt, Officer Teller," he said, "I and my fellow agents were busy doing real police work and, as usual, it paid off with real results. We've located the boyfriend, apprehended him, and gotten him to confess to the murder of Michael Lake. So you can go back to patrolling the highways for which at least you have some training."

Ray, who was standing behind Lucy and whose mouth was right by her ear, growled loud enough so only she could hear, "Witch hunt?"

Just as Lucy was going to congratulate Agent Scruggs through her clenched teeth, there was a knock on the door.

It was the receptionist. "Sorry for interrupting, but there is a man named Ezra Marsh out here who says he needs to talk with you, Lucy."

"Tell him I'm busy now. See if he'll talk with one of the other officers." Lucy sounded curt, but secretly she was glad to have a few more moments to compose herself so that her praise of Agent Scruggs could sound more sincere.

"I tried that," the receptionist answered in a shaky voice. "He says he'll only talk with you, and it has to do with the murder of Michael Lake."

"Maybe he was a witness," Scruggs enthused. "With the confession and a witness, we can put this thing to bed. Tell him you'll talk to him. We'll watch through the two-way mirror while you speak with him in the interrogation room."

Lucy started to say that she wasn't sure it was going to happen that way, but decided to go along with Scruggs's plan.

She was right: something very different happened.

Lucy took a deep breath and opened the door to the interrogation room. She smiled an informal greeting. "Ezra, it's good to see you again. You left the other night before we had a chance to thank you for helping Bobbie. I'm sure you saved her life. We would never have found her in time. We all appreciate your helping her."

Lieutenant Moon, standing outside the interrogation room behind the two-way mirror, looked over his glasses at Ray.

Ray looked back. "We haven't had a chance to write a report on that one yet, sir," he said briskly. Then Ray turned his attention back to the other side of the glass, in an effort to divert the Lieutenant's attention.

"Well, before anyone else gets hurt, I think it's time we end this. I know you're on to me. I'm here to confess to the murder of Michael Lake." His voice was getting softer, almost to a whisper.

This time the Lieutenant looked over his glasses at Agent Scruggs, who pretended not to notice. Like Ray, Scruggs kept his attention focused on the other side of the mirror.

"I'm confused for a lot of reasons," Lucy said, and leaned closer over the table. "One, because we already have someone who confessed to that murder, and two, what makes you think we even suspect you, much less have a case against you? All you've done is help us."

"I've heard people talk about you. I know you've lost your children temporarily because of alcohol, just like I almost lost my child. You've been straight for a couple of years. You would never risk losing them because you need a drink to warm up. You knew when you asked me for that drink that it wasn't whiskey in that bottle."

Now Lieutenant Moon didn't bother to look at anyone; he just rolled his eyes. He'd read Lucy's report, and obviously a few details had been left out.

"Well, I'm glad you have so much confidence in my sobriety, Ezra. I wish I did, but that still doesn't tell me why I should suspect you."

"You can talk with Karen. She'll tell you I used to abuse my daughter and my wife. I never got help for it. I just stopped. When my wife died, I just snapped. I needed to take my rage out on someone. I thought, who better than a child nobody wanted and was useless to the world anyway. So I took the baby and beat it to death. Then I burned the body and threw the ashes in the woods where no one would ever find them. I wanted that useless mother and her boyfriend to suffer the way I had suffered." His eyes began to fill with tears.

"You should have kept your mouth shut," said Lucy, "because the boyfriend has already confessed to the murder."

Agent Scruggs walked away from behind the two-way mirror without saying a word. The next anyone saw of him, he was opening the door to the interrogation room. "I'll take over from here, Officer Teller."

"I don't want to talk with you," said Ezra. "I want to talk with Lucy."

"Oh, I'm sorry, but you're a confessed murderer, and we usually don't give them a lot of choices about things. I'm FBI Agent Scruggs, and murder on the reservation is a federal crime, so you'll talk with me."

Then he turned to Lucy. "You need to leave before you end up losing our chance to convict anyone in this case," he told her.

Scruggs turned back to Ezra. "Now let me get this straight. Your wife died so you went to the trouble of kidnapping a child you didn't know in order to get even. Why not just shoot the doctor or the nurses who cared for your wife? How did you even know about this kid anyway?" Scruggs looked at Ezra and waited for an answer, but Ezra just stared back, comfortable in the silence.

Scruggs waited briefly, then he started up again. "You know what I think?" He paused briefly but again got nothing. "I think you're trying to get the boyfriend off the hook, or maybe you're friends with Officer Teller and want to make her look good."

There was a pause. Then Ezra spoke, and his voice was sulkily apologetic. "You're just too smart for us, Agent Scruggs. I was trying to help my buddy, but you got the right guy. Sorry I tried to pull the wool over your eyes."

"You know we could charge you with obstructing justice?"

"If you let me go, I'll testify against the boyfriend at the trial."

"You've got yourself a deal," Scruggs said with a smile.

Lucy, now standing on the other side of the two-way mirror, smiled too. She couldn't let this stand, but it bought her some time, and now it was with the blessing of the FBI.

As Ezra left the interrogation room he ran into a Native man in leg irons and handcuffs being escorted to a holding cell.

Then Ezra's tone changed again. "Now you are going to pay for the lives you've ruined with your chemicals, Bill Blackhawk," he barked.

Bill looked at him with bewilderment, then watched the retreating back of the angry man for as long as his guards would let him.

After Scruggs left, and with a great deal of trepidation, Ray and Lucy explained to Lieutenant Moon what they thought was really going on. He didn't look over his glasses at them; he just smiled throughout their explanation. Nothing pleased him more than making the FBI look foolish.

chapter 20

LUCY WENT RIGHT TO Karen's office. She was feeling unusually energized. She guessed it was partly the excitement of working with Ray and the Lieutenant. Something had definitely changed. She felt, in spite of her blunders as a police officer, that the Lieutenant respected her more. Even more importantly, she wasn't sure how Ray felt, but she knew she felt energy around him she hadn't experienced in years.

At one time, she had taken a family sociology class, and the instructor had talked about a chemical with a long name that she couldn't remember and never could pronounce, abbreviated as PEA—something your body produced only when you fell in love. It had the combined properties of speed and hallucinogens. It lasted in the body for only a short while, and no matter what the individual or couple did, the body stopped producing it after three or four years. The instructor's point was that if a couple was going to maintain a relationship, they needed to find other ways to keep their interest in one another. Lucy wasn't ready to admit to love yet, but her body was definitely trying to tell her something about Ray.

She was lucky enough when she reached Karen's office to find her there. Karen smiled when she saw Lucy. "Where do we start?" she asked.

"So much has happened on my end, I don't even know where to begin," Lucy replied. "I guess the bottom line is that Dawn's boyfriend confessed to killing Michael, and Ezra tried to confess to killing him, but the FBI didn't want to compromise their case. There's more to it, but I can fill you in as needed when I hear what happened on your end."

"Well," said Karen, "this time Ezra's daughter, Gabby, lived up to her name. I think she was so relieved to be able to talk to someone, she couldn't hold back. She said her father brought the baby over two days after he abducted him. She told her father to return the child, but he would have none of it. She admitted she didn't try too hard to convince him, and within days she began to see a difference in the baby's responsiveness. She promised she wouldn't do anything foolish but admitted it would be hard to give the baby up. She was particularly worried that Dawn would go back to using. I assured her that I would do what I could to keep her and Ezra both from getting in trouble, and if Dawn didn't improve, Gabby'd still be the first person I'd choose to care for Michael. What do we do next?"

"Well, the first thing I want to do is let Dawn know her baby's alive, and let Lisa and Dawn see the baby. Then I'll have to spring Dawn's boyfriend, and we may have to pick up Ezra."

"I'd like to go with you to talk with Dawn and to see the baby."

"That's great. I'd like your support."

So Lucy and Karen headed to Shawano. They picked up Lisa from school and met Gabby at her house. She greeted them at the door and offered them coffee and a soft drink for Lisa. Michael was taking a nap. Lisa looked anxious to see her brother, but waited patiently for the baby to wake. Lucy wondered how to bring up the abduction, but she didn't need to worry. As soon as they were all seated, Gabby started the discussion.

"Have you ever heard of the Birkebeiner, Officer Teller?"

"Is that that race they have in northwest Wisconsin?"

"That's a version of it. Have you ever heard the history of it?"

"No, I can't say as I have."

"The hardest time for my dad after he quit drinking was the winter. The bitter cold days he couldn't get out. He used to ice fish, but that was such a trigger for him to drink, he gave it up. Eventually, he found two things that helped him through. He used to help me with my homework, and he found a great interest in history and geography.

"He started reading things—books and magazines—that interested him. When I went off to college near Cable where the Birkebeiner is held, I think my parents followed more to find a bigger library than to be close to me. There my dad found another interest to keep him busy in the winter: cross-country skiing. He could still be out in the nature he loved and allow it to heal him, and he wasn't tempted to drink, because he didn't associate skiing with alcohol. He'd go out and burn off energy in the day and read till he fell asleep at night.

"He got so good he was even able to complete the thirty-six-mile Birkebeiner race. After my mother died, he'd spend the summers cutting narrow paths through the woods—too narrow for snowmobilers—so he could ski alone on them. One day, I made the mistake of complaining to him about Michael and how his life was in danger and how attached I had become to him.

"A few days later, he told me the story of the origin of the Birkebeiner. It seems the term came from a group of soldiers in Norway in 1296. They were called that because they wrapped skins around their legs in the winter and secured them with birch roots. 'Birkebeiner' means 'birch legs' in Norwegian.

"At that time in Norway, there was a civil war being fought between two kings. One of the kings died, and his heir was only two years old. The other king sent soldiers to kill the child, but the birch legs got wind of it and took the boy in a backpack from Lillehammer across the mountains to Rena—thirty-six miles. The little boy was named Haakon Haakonsson, and he grew up to unite Norway and bring it years of prosperity. They have the race in Norway every year to commemorate the heroism of the birch legs, but in Norway, the six thousand racers must also wear a three-and-a-half-kilo backpack as a symbol of the child that was saved by the birch legs.

"When my father told me that story, I thought he was just telling me a story about something he read. I had almost forgotten about it until he showed up at my house in the middle of the night with Michael. To you, my father is a kidnapper, but to him, he's a birch leg soldier saving a young prince from harm."

Lucy was getting ready to answer when she heard a baby's cry from the other room. She looked over at Karen. Lucy had seen her cry only one other time, and that was when Lucy first entered treatment and Karen brought her to visit her kids for the first time. Now the tears were streaming down the other woman's face.

Lisa had sat and listened quietly until she heard the baby cry; then she jumped and looked eagerly toward the cry. Gabby noticed right away.

"Lisa," she said, "would you like to go with me while I get Michael up from his nap?"

Lisa nodded and even smiled. She hurried to follow Gabby to his bedroom. The three of them came back together just a few minutes later. Lisa couldn't take her eyes off Michael. Lucy was seeing him for the first time and was surprised how responsive he seemed to be for a baby who everyone thought had so many problems. Karen asked if she could hold him, and her eyes quickly filled with tears again.

His eyes were bright and he seemed alert. He responded warmly to touch. Lisa was sitting down again but still watching her brother. Gabby asked her if she wanted to hold him, and she smiled and nodded her head. Perhaps it was coincidence, but Michael put his hand on her cheek in a gesture that looked to all in the room like, "Thanks, big sister. You've been my salvation."

"I'd like to take Michael to see his mother in the treatment center," Lucy said, looking compassionately at Gabby. "I promise I'll have him back in a few hours."

Gabby just nodded. "I'll get him dressed. Lisa, come help me."

Lisa followed Gabby into Michael's bedroom.

When they left, Karen just shook her head over and over. "I can't believe the change in that child. Loving people can do miracles," she said.

Little did they know, the real miracle of love was yet to come.

chapter 21

MICHAEL WAS A HUGE hit at the treatment center. The nurses and even Dr. Meany huddled around Dawn when Lucy put Michael in her arms. Dawn started to cry the moment she saw him.

"My baby has emerged from a frigid winter with a new soul," she said through her tears. Then she began to speak directly to him: "Yes, Michael, I recognize your body, but your soul is new."

Dr. Wolf, ever mindful of an opportunity for therapeutic intervention, said, "If Michael could talk, I bet he'd say, 'Right back at you, Mom.'"

Everyone laughed and applauded in recognition of the truth in that statement. Dawn, like Michael, had been transformed. Physically, she was so much healthier. Gone were the dark circles under her eyes, the puffiness of her face. Her hair was clean and shiny black. There were a lot more changes—changes that could not be seen visibly. Gone was the constipation and then diarrhea of withdrawal. Gone were the aches of her muscles and joints. With her kidneys working the way they should, she had lost a lot of water retention, and exercise was starting to restore her muscle tone.

That was nothing, though, compared to the changes she was making mentally, emotionally, socially, and spiritually. Gone was the whiny person who wanted to make everyone else responsible for her pain. She was out of her room now and participating in individual and group sessions. She was starting to come out of herself, recognizing and responding to the pain of others, but she was also confronting them with the behaviors she recognized as part of their own addiction and becoming increasingly discerning of her own addictive behavior. She no longer wanted to be left alone all the time and was beginning to socialize and laugh with patients and staff. Dr. Wolf told Lucy later that Dawn was the biggest star at the treatment center since Lucy herself had left.

It was as if Dawn and Michael had recognized each other for the first time. The instincts of motherhood had kicked in with Dawn, and Michael responded with all of the adorable cooing and babbling of a healthy ten-month-old. He was sitting up without support and he was aware of his surroundings. Mother and son looked at one another for a very long moment before Dawn gave him back to Karen.

"Will you watch him and Lisa while I talk to Lucy and Dr. Wolf?"

The three of them went to Dr. Wolf's office. "I wanted to speak to the two of you before I commit myself, but I'm thinking that maybe I should let Gabby keep Michael. I've seen her with him in the hospital, and she's great. I have my hands full with Lisa, and I need to focus on recovery. Besides, I've had my chance with him, and I blew it. Perhaps Lisa and I could pick him up on the weekends sometimes. When he was missing, I made a deal with God that if he were just alive, I'd find a better home for him. I know I couldn't find a better home than the one he's in now."

Lucy and Dr. Wolf sat in silence for a while—partly from shock, partly sorting out all that was being said and letting the thoughts flow over them. They gave silence a chance to sort out the magnitude of what they had just heard.

Dr. Wolf spoke first. "I think the idea is admirable, and I'm even more impressed that you didn't just blurt it out with others around—you were able to make the decision to keep it private. You really are getting better. I think it is such an important decision that we should leave it here with the three of us, and we should all continue to think about it. You still have some time in treatment and then months of aftercare and perhaps a halfway house. We don't have to decide this today."

"I think that's a great idea, Dr. Wolf," said Lucy. "But on the other hand, the longer that we leave Michael with Gabby, the more attached they will become to one another, and separating them again will become more and more painful. I don't think we should put this off too long."

They agreed to meet again before Dawn left treatment. Lucy also got permission from Dawn to have Lisa see a psychologist. Dawn granted it without hesitation.

On the way back, Lucy had to struggle to keep from sharing Dawn's thoughts with Karen, but she knew she couldn't. They had to be careful not to discuss anything too openly; Lisa was there. Karen was wrestling with the same thing.

After they dropped Lisa off, Karen began talking almost immediately. "After seeing Michael with Gabby," she said, "I was convinced I would fight to give her custody, but then I saw Michael with Dawn. Maybe it is time for me to retire. I'm getting too old for this. Or I'm getting too soft for this."

"Maybe we need to let God work it out," said Lucy. "We have some time before we need to make that decision. I'm sure glad that Dawn isn't on an insurance company's plan. She probably would have been moved to outpatient treatment after five days and that would have been devastating. I think that one reason Dr. Wolf stays on the reservation is that he doesn't have to fight with insurance companies every day to get people what they need. I think he'll keep her there as long as he can."

After dropping off Karen, Lucy stopped in to see Lieutenant Moon. She told him the news that what they had suspected was proved true: that Michael was still alive. He took great pleasure in calling to inform Agent Scruggs of that fact, and he and Lucy laughed together at the long pause on the other end of the line when he got the news.

chapter *22*

DURING THE SCOTT Brandt case, Lucy took Lisa to a psychologist. The visit helped Lisa to verbalize the trauma she had experienced when her teacher Mr. Reilly, now in jail, had taken pictures of her naked.

Now, as her new case unfolded, Lucy didn't forget Lisa's trauma. She didn't need help interpreting Lisa's account of Michael's kidnapping; Hank had done that. But she knew all the help Lisa would need, especially with the added trauma of Michael's disappearance, and brought her back to see the psychologist.

The psychologist again allowed Lucy to watch through the two-way mirror, as she engaged in play therapy with Lisa. Lucy had made a point of doing a paper on it for a psychology class she was taking, after her last experience with it.

Lucy remembered clearly all that the psychologist had told her the first time: "It's difficult to get even normal children to talk and it's especially hard after a trauma. Often they communicate best through play. They gain mastery through their play and they tend to focus on the things that traumatize them. If a child has been in a car accident they'll crash cars together over and over again. If they've been physically abused, they'll take a doll and hit it again and again. If they've been sexually abused they'll focus on the genitals of the doll."

As Lucy looked through the two-way mirror she again saw the room full of toys, but the psychologist didn't direct Lisa toward any of them particularly. There were a number of dolls in the room; some were dolls that looked like babies, but others were grown-up dolls that could take the part of Mommy and Daddy and other adults in Lisa's life. Just as she had last time, Lisa picked up the toy camera in the room, and she was soon taking pictures of everything, once again focusing on the dolls. After taking pictures for a while she dropped the camera and picked up a baby doll.

"Would you like me to take the part of the baby?" the psychologist asked.

"No," Lisa answered, "he and his sister are going to sleep now. You be the witch who takes the baby."

The psychologist, knowing the story, took some face paint and painted her face and put her briefcase on her back, held there by a shoulder strap. When she picked up the baby, Lisa lifted up the girl doll and speaking for her said, "Hey, where are you going with my brother?"

"I'm going off into the night and you may never see him again. You must stay here and protect your mother. I have put her in a deep sleep."

"You are too big and powerful for me, witch. I want to help my brother, but what will happen to mother?" Lisa said, still speaking through the doll.

"Trust my powerful magic, and maybe you will all be better," the witch answered.

"But I miss my brother," Lisa answered starting to cry. "I don't want to play anymore," she said though her tears.

Lucy came in from the observation room and held her as she cried.

"I think that is enough for today," the psychologist said.

Once again, Lucy began to offer prayers for herself and for Lisa. Though her mother and children had done what they could to make Lisa welcome in their home, Lisa still had the lost look of a child overwhelmed with changes. A new home— new caregivers—and her mother, father, and brother all gone were taking their toll on her.

The psychologist suggested that Lucy look for someone who could fill Scott's role in Lisa's life. Lucy mentioned Kathy, but the psychologist suggested a young male might be better in encouraging Lisa to transfer her feelings for Scott. After discussing it with Ray, he suggested Mike Sanipaw. Mike had been Ray's partner on the police force for quite some time and Ray said he trusted him with his life, which he often did. He was tall and good-looking like Scott and had the same charm with children.

The next day Ray brought him by for dinner, and Lisa's eyes immediately brightened, and in the kitchen she asked Lucy if she could sit next to him at dinner. After dinner Mike asked Lisa if he could help with her homework, and though she had told Lucy earlier she didn't have any homework, she soon produced a stack of books she needed help with.

Before he left, he asked Lisa to go to a Disney movie showing in Shawano over the weekend, and she acted like she was invited to the prom by a movie star.

"Thanks, Mike, you're the best. It's no wonder all the single women on the rez are waiting in line for you," Lucy teased as she and Ray walked him to his car.

"You should know what that is like because every single male envies Ray," Mike shot back with a smile.

Next, Lucy went to talk with Bill Blackhawk, who was still in custody.

Lucy was prepared to dislike him; he was responsible for Dawn's addiction to heroin, and fed the addiction by keeping her supplied. His record as a father to Lisa and Michael showed more neglect than abuse, as damaging to young children as physical violence. She expected him to be violently angry, especially at her.

But Lucy was surprised. Though she could tell he was still suffering from withdrawal symptoms, the first thing he did was thank Lucy for what she was doing for his family.

"You'll be happy to know that Michael is still alive," she said in response. "Why did you confess to a murder you didn't commit?"

It took Bill awhile to stop crying so he could answer. "Figured that Dawn had somehow done it accidentally and then panicked and dumped the body somewhere. I feel so guilty for what I've done to her and those children that it was the least

I could do to protect her. As for my life, it doesn't amount to anything anyway. So what difference does it make?"

Lucy just listened quietly.

"What happened to the baby? And how did you find him?"

"I can't tell you too much about that because it's an ongoing investigation. I can tell you that Michael was kidnapped and taken to a safe place by someone who was concerned for his welfare. You'll be happy to know that Michael is doing quite well where he is and has started to function appropriately for his age level."

"Does this mean I'm free to go?"

"Yes, but I have a favor to ask you."

"What's that?"

"I'd like you either to enter treatment the way Dawn did or leave the area. I think Dawn has a real chance of staying straight, but if you reenter her life and you're using, you'll take her with you. You both will lose everything, even your lives."

Lucy appreciated the fact that Bill thought long and hard about what she had asked. He didn't answer her right away. He just sat there silently in his cell. Lucy gave him all the time he needed to think.

When he finally spoke, unusual sincerity was on his face. "I love Dawn and those kids, in spite of what you might think," he said. "I don't just use her, although it probably appears that way. But I don't know if I can stop using."

"I'm not asking for promises," Lucy assured him. "You've already gone through the worst of withdrawal. When I let you go, instead of stopping at your dealer, go to treatment. Give it a try."

"Would you take me to the treatment center to see Dawn? I don't really trust myself. I know if I leave here now, I don't have the strength to pass up heroin."

Lucy drove him to Maehnowesekiyah. Dawn was surprised to see him and hugged him warmly. They talked, but only for a few minutes.

"Where's Michael?" Bill asked, almost immediately.

"With Gabby," Dawn replied. Then she told him about Gabby and their son. "I'm thinking of giving her custody," she concluded.

After that, he was more restless and edgy than he had been in the prison cell.

Lucy was hoping he'd stay and allow Dr. Wolf to admit him, but he said he had some business to take care of first.

"A score to settle," he said.

Lucy worried he meant scoring some heroin but, really, Bill was thinking of another score.

The next day, when she received a panic-stricken call from Gabby, it seems that her worst fears had been realized. She called Ray in as backup and headed over to face the horrifying new development.

Bill Blackhawk didn't go looking for heroin as Lucy suspected but his mind was still in its grasp.

At first, when Dawn told him about Michael and Gabby, Bill was silent. He was thinking of his brief encounter with Ezra and putting two and two together. Unhappy, faced with the knowledge of all he had done wrong, however much he was in denial, Bill wanted to work off his anger in some way. He decided Ezra would pay for what he had done to his family.

His first thought was to take the baby back from Gabby. When Lucy left the room for a moment to speak to some of the treatment center staff, he got Gabby's number from Dawn.

As soon as he had a chance, he called Gabby and asked if he could stop by and see the baby. Gabby agreed, but told him to stop by the next day in the afternoon when her father would be there.

"He never showed up," she told Lucy over the phone. "My father came and we all waited. My husband even arrived home. But there was no sign of Bill. Then my father left. A few minutes passed and someone broke into the garage and took one of our snowmobiles and raced after my father. I knew it must be Bill, and so I called you immediately."

Lucy and Ray drove her truck rapidly in chase. They arrived at the fire lane on VV just as Bill was crossing it.

They unloaded the snowmobiles and skis they had loaded into the back as quickly as possible, but Bill had a big lead and Ezra would be farther ahead—at least they hoped he would be.

Ezra had loaded up with supplies in Shawano while visiting his daughter. Reaching his garage, he unloaded the snowmobile and loaded his supplies onto a sled. He had just started off on his skis, dragging the laden sled behind him, when Bill arrived. He should have been a sitting duck for Bill, but though many people in Wisconsin were skilled on a snowmobile, Bill wasn't one of them. His recreation for the last several years had come at the end of a needle. He was heading straight for Ezra and could easily have hit him. But instead Bill swerved and hit a tree. The snowmobile stopped but he didn't. He twisted around in the air just enough to keep from hitting the tree head-on.

When Ray and Lucy arrived at Ezra's garage, they saw the snowmobile against the tree and blood near the tree and even more blood leading away from the tree. It was getting dark and they both turned on their headlamps, following the trail of blood until it got too dark to see.

Ray took the lead with his headlamp illuminating the trail and the edge of the woods. Their skiing had improved dramatically from that first day when they got lessons from Hank. Without the packs they had carried on their first day, and with a clear destination, they moved at twice the pace they did then.

At that moment, to Lucy, it was still way too slow. All she could think of was Bill and Ezra and whether they were alive. There was a lot that Lucy liked about being a cop, but dealing with death was something she hated. She had never gotten used to it. At times, she was haunted by the finality of it. Now she could only hurry and hope.

They skied silently through the night. Lucy thought of what she had been through just a month or two earlier. She thought about how tired she was then. She remembered vividly how her lip had throbbed where Reilly had hit her. She was reminded of the pain in her ribs, cracked where Kane had hit her. Even now, the pain in her chest increased with each deep breath she took as she exerted herself to move faster down the trail. She thought of Kathy and Brad. What if Kathy had died that night? What about Kathy's father who still wasn't over the death of his wife, and who had put everything into raising his daughter? What about Brad who finally had the chance to be with the one he had loved from afar for so long? They had all survived that night and the murderers had been charged and imprisoned. What would happen with this case?

She could now see a light coming from Ezra's cabin. To Lucy, it was a light of hope burning through the dark woods that surrounded them—like the tiny light of life that burns in each of us, too often unfairly forced out early by evil, a light that is so fragile and burns for just an instant in comparison to the life of the universe.

Those tense final minutes were the worst. Ezra's light didn't seem to get any closer. Occasionally the light disappeared when a larger tree would block it from view.

Finally they arrived outside of the cabin.

"Ezra, are you in there?" Lucy shouted.

His voice came back faintly. "Yes, but I'm busy at the moment, so just let yourselves in."

Ray and Lucy skied the additional distance to the cabin and quickly removed their skis. When they entered, the first thing they saw was Bill lying on the kitchen table, his bloody clothes torn open and even more blood across his body. Ezra was bending over him. On the table alongside the unconscious man was some rubbing alcohol and a bottle of whiskey.

Great, Lucy thought. Ezra is operating on Bill, and he's drunk on top of it.

Though wanting to hold back for fear of what she would see, Lucy rushed over. Ezra never looked up, but as she approached and stood next to him, he spoke softly. "You guys arrived just in time. I've been looking all over this cabin for a pair of scissors to cut these stitches, and I can't find one. You don't have a Swiss army knife on you, do you?"

Ray pulled one from his pocket and handed it to Lucy.
"Great. When I tell you, cut the thread."

Lucy looked down at Bill and saw that Ezra had removed his coat and sweater and had placed several clean stitches in a three-inch-long gash in his side. Bill looked pale and didn't appear to be conscious. Ray put his arm around Lucy when he noticed she had become pale too. Still not looking up, Ezra said, "I think your friend will be okay. He's lost some blood, but the tree just grazed his head and his side."

Ezra showed Lucy where to cut the thread, and then Ray raised Bill up while Ezra wrapped a bandage made from a pillowcase around his waist. They covered him with one of Ezra's flannel shirts and moved him to the nearby bed.

"Has he passed out from loss of blood?" Lucy asked.

"I would say he's more likely passed out from the alcohol I gave him."

"Where did you get the whiskey?" Lucy said, struggling to keep the distress out of her voice. "I can tell it's not the pretend stuff you had the last time we were out here."

"You know, God works in mysterious ways. I haven't had a drink in twenty years, and on the way back with your friend, I found a bottle in a hollow tree that I must have hid during a blackout. Finally, something good has come from those days."

"What happened out there?" Lucy asked.

"I had just gotten off my sled, and put on my skis and loaded the provisions onto the sled and hooked it to my waist. I was a sitting duck for Bill to hit me with the snowmobile, but at the last second he veered off and hit a tree. He was lying in the snow and bleeding pretty bad. I told him I'd fix him up if he agreed to get help and be the husband and father he was capable of, or I'd let him bleed to death in the snow. I guess recovery looked like a good alternative to him—at the time, anyway. I put some snow on his wounds to slow the bleeding, and then I put him on the sled I pull behind my skis and told him to keep his hand against his side and one at the side of his head. When I found the bottle, I gave him a few good belts to ease the pain. It seemed to start working right away.

"He would come in and out of consciousness and we'd talk sometimes. I suggested he not do it the way I did, that he should get some help. Since I was invested in him now, I'd even go to meetings with him, even be his sponsor if he wanted. You know, I've had some amazing discoveries living out here alone. You guys have all of those cell phones and text messages that I see in TV commercials when I visit my daughter, but I tune into different channels out here—spiritual ones. But now I think it's time for me to connect with the living again. Maybe I can help Dawn and Bill and Lisa to survive and find a new life."

Lucy smiled.

"Could we use that sled to get him to the snowmobiles we have by your garage and get him to a hospital?" Ray asked.

"Sure," said Ezra. "I'll get my coat and pull him for you."

They bundled Bill up in a coat and blanket. He woke up briefly and smiled when he saw Lucy and Ray.

"You are about to have a rough ride," Ezra said, and gave him a few more sips of whiskey.

"Careful with that stuff, Ezra," said Lucy. "He will need to detox all over again." She added, as if in an afterthought, "And, maybe you too."

"Hell," said Ezra with a short laugh, "years ago I would have had it drained ten minutes after I found it. Now I would rather drink battery acid than that stuff. I'm going to die sober."

"Glad to hear you say that, Ezra, but all I say is I'm not going to drink today."

"Well, if you drink tomorrow," said Ezra, "I might have to come and take those beautiful children of yours."

"They are the reason I will get up tomorrow morning and say I'm not going to drink today."

"Why not get it all out of the way at once like I did?"

"You will have to come to a meeting with me sometime and I'll let the experts explain that."

"Maybe I'll just do that. I've pretty much promised Bill I will if he wants me to. I don't think they will influence me much, but I do get lonely out here sometimes, and I could use the fellowship."

Once Bill was safely in the sled, Ezra took off toward the fire lane. Even pulling a sled, he moved so quickly that Ray and Lucy could barely keep up with him. Once they reached the fire lane, they attached the sled to one of the snowmobiles and drove to VV. There was an ambulance waiting at VV with its dome lights flashing.

Bill opened his eyes and looked at all the commotion with even more confusion.

"You people in AA, don't you say when your day is going bad that you need a 'do over'?" He laughed and cringed at the pain. "Well, this is a real 'do over' for me, I think."

Lucy and Ray waited at the hospital nearly an hour while Bill was admitted for observation. Once they got into his room, they all had little to say. Bill had a tube in each arm, one with an antibiotic and the other with blood.

"Do you remember the promise you made to Ezra?" Lucy asked Bill.

"I remember and I plan to keep it. As soon as I get out of here I want to go where Dawn is. I want to get better, and when I get out of there I'm going to drag his ass to a meeting. He's going to pay for every stitch in my head and side."

Ray and Lucy looked at one another and smiled. The case of the Witch of Winter and the missing boy seemed to be concluding happily for everyone.

LUCY THOUGHT THAT
Agent Scruggs would just want this whole case to disappear,
but to her surprise he pursued it, issuing a warrant for Ezra's
arrest. He listed on the warrant not only kidnapping, but also
child endangerment.

Lucy was disappointed. She had hoped it could all go
away.

She and Ray were given the assignment of serving the
warrant and arresting Ezra. They set out the next morning in
snowmobiles and carrying their skis. Once she was on her skis,
Lucy's mind began wandering. She thought about the fact that
without Ezra, she might never have started skiing. Now she
was quite sure she would continue. She was convinced that Ray
enjoyed it too. She was hoping that soon she could get her
children to try it.

It was a sunny day with the temperature in the twenties,
perfect for skiing. As she looked at the trees, she thought she
could see the shadow of spring buds on the branches. The snow

sparkled as if to say, "Stay in the moment. Don't wish me away. Appreciate the beauty that I offer."

But she had to struggle to enjoy that moment. Both she and Ray had brought their weapons, but she hoped and prayed it wouldn't come to using them. Ezra had been willing to confess once, but that was to protect his daughter and new grandson. She was quite sure Ezra would rather die than go to jail.

For a long time they skied in silence. Lucy wondered what Ray was thinking. Was he, too, thinking of Ezra? Or was he simply considering the beauty that surrounded them? She felt comfortable with the silence, but she admitted to herself that she wondered what was in his heart. Did he get the same strong feelings when he was around her that she got around him?

Soon they arrived at Ezra's cabin. Lucy saw smoke coming from his chimney. He must be home.

"Ezra, it's Lucy Teller and Ray Waupuse," Ray called. "Can we come and speak with you for a while?"

They waited respectfully for him to appear on his porch. It seemed like a long time, but the door finally opened, and he appeared.

"Come in. I'll make some coffee," he shouted and waved his arm in welcome.

Lucy and Ray skied to the porch. Then they took off their skis, propping them against the side of the house next to Ezra's which were still covered with snow. Then they entered the cabin. He must have spent the morning skiing, Lucy thought, then come back and lit a fire in the stove and lay down to take a nap until she and Ray had come and interrupted his dreams. The cabin still had a chill to it and Ezra's bed looked like he had just vacated it. The three of them remained silent while Ezra brewed coffee and poured three cups.

"So what brings you two out here today?" he asked as he handed them each a cup that steamed excessively in the still chilly air. "It gets so a guy can't get through his daily routine anymore without getting interrupted by the police."

Lucy could imagine the daily routine he meant: a morning spent skiing and hunting, then lunch, followed by a nap. She imagined he frequently went to Loon Lake to have dinner with his daughter and her family. Then he would sled and ski back to his cabin in the dark. She was choked up at the thought of what would happen to this man confined to an eight-by-six-foot jail cell.

Still, Lucy saw no way to soften the blow. "I'm afraid we have a warrant for your arrest, Ezra," she said.

Ezra took a deep breath and looked toward heaven. Lucy thought she heard him murmur his wife's name: "Emily."

Then there was a long silence. Finally, Ezra shook his head.

"I don't understand white man's law. Because of what I did, Michael has a better home and a better life ahead. His mother got the help she needed. His dad did too. Hank and Bobbie got a chance to relieve some of their grief and guilt. You two had a chance to spend time together and fall in love, whether you know it or not, and I got a chance to work on my grief and loss. For this, I should be punished?

"The only thing I did that I should be punished for is scaring you guys. That's the only thing I regret."

"I agree," said Ray.

"Then how can you guys do this?" His eyes searched for some answers.

"A person who has higher authority than we do has ordered us to bring you in to stand trial," Lucy answered.

"How can there be a higher authority than your own conscience?"

Lucy and Ray looked at each other.

"Just let me put on my skis and head into the woods. Give me a gun with one bullet in it, and I'll save the taxpayers the cost of a trial and prison. I'll be with Emily and all will be well."

"I would strongly consider that," said Lucy, "except for two reasons: one, I have a line of people who are ready to testify on your behalf. White man's justice is blind perhaps, but they sometimes have a heart when it comes to sentencing. I don't think you will get any jail time. Second, you are one of the few men in the world who might be able to say you delivered a baby. I want you to live to enjoy Michael."

Lucy had said the magic words.

"I'll be ready in a minute," Ezra said and turned to dress for his trip.

LUCY'S PREDICTIONS WERE realized, as were many of her hopes.

The judge and the district attorney agreed that Ezra was not a flight risk. A group of people including Hank, Kathy, Ray, and Gabby came up with bail.

The trial went as Lucy predicted. Those testifying on Ezra's behalf included Karen, Lucy, Dawn, Bill, Ray, Hank, and Bobbie. Ezra was found guilty of kidnapping, but the judge sentenced him to probation and community service.

Ezra was good to his word and visited Bill in treatment. Together they started attending meetings. Ezra even took a group of the alumni from treatment to Garski Flowage between Langlade and Antigo. There they met Hank, his family, and some friends and spent the day cross-country skiing and picnicking in the warming house there. Just as Lucy had expected, Doc Wolf loved the skiing. He even brought his son and daughter who were home from college for the weekend. Lucy was surprised that his wife, Gayle, didn't join them.

"She said she didn't want to spend the day freezing her butt off and watching me get addicted to another form of exercise. She decided on the casino instead," Doc said, with a hint of disappointment. "The kids are having a great time, though, so maybe this is one I won't have to do alone."

Maybe Gayle better worry about her own addictions if she decides on the casino instead of being with her family, Lucy thought, but she thought better of saying it. Dr. Wolf didn't seem quite his calm, friendly self. She wondered if he was a little uncomfortable playing a different role than he was used to with his patients.

Ezra seemed to get along well with the group and talked about attending other functions that the group offered.

Kathy and Brad were there too. Lucy had not seen Brad since Scott's funeral, but being close to Kathy meant knowing about Brad. Their relationship had deepened quickly and Lucy was not surprised to see a modest engagement ring on Kathy's finger.

"It may seem sudden," said Kathy quickly. "But it isn't really."

"No," said Lucy. "I know it isn't."

Kathy looked relieved. She smiled. "I knew you would understand, Lucy," she said. "The Brandts understand too. Everyone understands, really. I was afraid that someone would think it was wrong or disloyal to Scott."

Lucy shook her head with a smile. "No, I think Scott would be happy to see how well everyone is doing. And I think that he is happy about you and Brad."

Kathy, with tears in her eyes, hugged Lucy.

The biggest surprise of the day was that Agent Scruggs also joined the group. In spite of his stiff external appearance, he was a good athlete and very quickly picked up skiing and even ventured into the expert runs. Lucy sat with him while they warmed up and had some snacks at the lodge.

"You know," Scruggs said to her, unprompted, "when I was first given this assignment, I was a new agent right out of the Air Force. I hated the whole thing. I thought I'd be wasting my time and talent up here, but actually I've learned a lot from being here. I've come to appreciate nature and all it has to offer. We would all benefit from spending more time like we are spending it today. But I've learned the most from you, Officer Teller. There is much more to police work than you can learn from a book or the academies. You have a feel for people that no one could teach."

Lucy swallowed and thanked Jim Scruggs sincerely. "That may be true, but I have to admit too that I misjudged you. I appreciate your coming today so I could get to know you. Not many people in your position would do this."

"Maybe that's why so many in my position are out of touch with what really matters in the world," he replied. Then he smiled. "Of course," he added, "I hope next time we meet maybe I'll do the right thing and not look so foolish."

chapter *27*

EVEN THOUGH SHE
was going to be in a wedding later that day, Kathy didn't miss
her morning run. It was fall, sunny but cold, and Kathy was
appreciating every moment. She watched each breath leave
her body like puffs from a steam engine. The weatherman had
predicted a day in the sixties if the sunshine held. Right now,
there wasn't a cloud in the sky, but the prediction still seemed
like a stretch.

Still, Kathy wasn't complaining. It was sunny and brilliant.
She had parked her car at Lucy's house on Rabbit Ridge Road,
as they had planned to dress together. Lucy was excited at the
prospect from the moment Kathy proposed it. Getting ready
with Kathy was like preparing for the prom she had never
attended.

Kathy followed the path Lucy had told her to follow, up
Old South Branch Road and turning off at the sand and gravel
road after the hill and the curve. As she continued through a

field filled with the gold, brown, and orange of fall, she noticed a familiar figure next to a large tree.

Kathy stopped running and waited respectfully as Lucy completed her smudging ceremony. When the smoke had subsided and Lucy had returned the items to her bag, Kathy spoke.

"I was thinking about some perfume today, too, but I'm thinking of a little different fragrance."

Lucy smiled and stood quickly. The two women hugged.

"I suppose at a wedding you have the right to act like a girly girl," Lucy teased.

They ran off through the woods together.

Lucy had dated Ray Waupuse for several months now. Her children liked him, as did her mother, but Lucy continued to be cautious.

Ray was not demanding. In fact, Lucy thought he was pretty cautious himself about taking on a wife and two children—not to mention a wife one drink away from serious problems. Lucy's program was strong and getting stronger, but the reality of addiction was all around Ray, particularly in his line of work.

The biggest problem for Lucy was getting used to a man so different from any she had known so intimately. He was kind, gentle, and considerate and even after two years of working with him, she found herself doubting he was real. Despite all her experience with men, Lucy couldn't explain why she was attracted to him. But there was no denying she was.

Lucy had changed direction in school and now majored in special education. She had felt it was the right choice from the time she had seen Scott's students at his funeral, and in the weeks spent with Lisa, she was convinced. She was even helped by a scholarship set up by the Brandt family to which several people who attended the funeral had contributed.

She would never forget the speech Hank Brandt made at the medal ceremony where they presented her with the scholarship.

"You came as close as humanly possible to giving us our son back," he said. Then he added something that perhaps only she fully understood. "We thought our son had died wrapped up in his addiction to snow, but because of your work and the risks you took, we now know our son was involved in protecting the fragile yellow butterflies in his charge. I and my family will always be grateful for that."

After the ceremony, he thanked her again, this time for the opportunity she had allowed him to help in finding Michael.

"You could still be the maid of honor," Kathy said, as she pulled Lucy back from her thoughts. They had started running back to town together. They had discovered earlier on a run that neither of them had to change their pace for the other.

"You have a maid of honor. Besides, I already have one gown I will never wear again. I don't need two."

"My maid of honor never saved my life, and you can take her place in jeans if you want."

"You still don't get the concept. My stupidity almost cost you your life once. I didn't save it. Maybe Ray could be your mister of honor."

"Well, I guess I'll have to settle for the fact that you'll both be there."

"Of course I'll be there. Weddings seem to be cluttering up my social calendar all of a sudden—a wedding today and then your wedding... I don't have time for anything else!"

"Well," said Kathy, laughing, "I'm thankful that you're coming to the wedding and for the friendship we've developed."

Lucy smiled at her, and as their legs continued to move in harmony, she put her arm around Kathy's shoulder for a moment. No words were necessary.

They finished their run in silence. When they got to Lucy's house, Lucy went inside to pay her respects to Kathy's father, whom Kathy had brought with her. He had been talking with Lucy's mother and children.

"How are you doing, Uncle?" she asked in the traditional greeting toward an elder. "I hear you will be expanding your family soon."

"It helps for me to think of it that way."

Lucy smiled a sad smile knowing all too well what it was like to have the soul of your house missing. She patted his knee, knowing there were no words.

"Well, I better check on Ray and start getting ready. I don't dress up a lot, so I don't have much practice. Come to think of it, neither does Ray. I'm sure he'll want my help. He doesn't wear a suit very often."

Lucy called Ray and talked with him, then gave the phone to Kathy to talk with Brad who was getting ready at Ray's.

They all talked and laughed. It was, Lucy decided, exactly like kids getting ready for the prom. Lucy began thinking about what it would be like to plan a wedding of her own.

Kathy handed the phone back to Lucy. Ray was laughing into the phone and teasing her. Her planning increased a notch and her hopes for the future grew even more real.

LISA AND MICHAEL'S parents, Dawn and Bill, had both been straight for over six months. They both attended AA and aftercare at the treatment center. Lisa stayed with Lucy and her family for a month after Bill finished treatment to give them all time to adjust to living clean and sober. Michael remained with Gabby. His new grandpa, Ezra, looked forward to teaching him about the outdoors. Bill and Dawn had given him up for adoption and with Karen's help, the process went smoothly. They visited Gabby and Michael occasionally and the arrangement seemed to be working well.

Bill asked Dawn to marry him after three months of sobriety. Their counselors at the center warned them about making big changes in their lives with less than a year of sobriety under their belts, but since they had lived together for years, even the counselors had to admit it wasn't that big of a change. Since they didn't have a lot of sober friends after years of using, Dawn asked Lucy, Kathy, and Bobbie to be her bridesmaids.

And Bill asked Ray, Brad, and Tom, Bobbie's boyfriend, to be his groomsmen.

Lucy, Bobbie, and Kathy drove in Lucy's truck over to St. Michael's Catholic Church. Their families came separately. After the wedding, they planned to drive around town, then head for Legend Lake to take some outdoor photos. Lucy hoped to get some pictures with the loons or an eagle in the background. The eagle seemed to be an ever more powerful part in her life.

Father Dan performed the ceremony. The reception was modest but pleasant.

The quiet supper was almost finished when Brad, unprompted, rose to speak.

Lucy was surprised. Brad appeared to be such a quiet, shy man, but he seemed comfortable standing before them all. Brad spoke of wanting them to care for one another. Then he spoke of the three C's—Cultivate, Commit, and Communicate.

Father Dan stood up, laughingly apologizing for talking again outside the pulpit, and picked right up on Brad's words.

"In some ways," he said, "words are like the seeds we plant and cultivate. Words can be used to inflict endless damage, or words can be used to heal. Your words can be weeds that choke and destroy life, or your words can nurture and enhance life. Your words can be seeds that create or destroy. Think of the possibility that every word out of your mouth is a seed or a weed. Let's each of us choose today, in honor of all the people here now and those who attend in spirit, to plant seeds of life."

Father Dan stopped and looked into every face in the room.

"Seeds or weeds, it's your choice. Plant seeds, people. Plant seeds."

Lucy looked over at Ray. This was someone with whom she hoped to be planting seeds on many different levels for a long time to come. She also looked at so many other people in the church who were all part of her life, and she hoped with all of them she could say and do things to cultivate and nourish them.